CROWNED BY MUSIC

"Here they are!"

Linetta then looked down and realised that standing opposite them on the other side of the wishing well were two men.

It took her a moment to realise that they were in uniform and were very obviously Russians.

As the Prince's fingers now tightened on hers, they were painful.

Then she heard him demand of the Russians,

"Who are you and what are you doing here?"

To her astonishment he did not speak in his own language but in German, which she had always understood the Russians used when they were moving about Europe and not in their own country.

"We have been looking for Your Royal Highness," one of the men replied. "And, as we've been so clever in finding you, we'll certainly be rewarded when we tell those who've sent us that your body lies at the bottom of this well from which it can never be recovered."

As he spoke, he pulled a gun from under his arm and the man beside him did the same.

It flashed through Linetta's mind that these men were about to kill the Prince and she felt the full horror of the moment and could only gasp.

Then she remembered the pistols which were in the pocket of her coat.

THE BARBARA CARTLAND
PINK COLLECTION

Titles in this series

CROWNED BY MUSIC

BARBARA CARTLAND

Barbaracartland.com Ltd

THE BARBARA CARTLAND PINK COLLECTION

Dame Barbara Cartland is still regarded as the most prolific bestselling author in the history of the world.

In her lifetime she was frequently in the Guinness Book of Records for writing more books than any other living author.

Her most amazing literary feat was to double her output from 10 books a year to over 20 books a year when she was 77 to meet the huge demand.

She went on writing continuously at this rate for 20 years and wrote her very last book at the age of 97, thus completing an incredible 400 books between the ages of 77 and 97.

Her publishers finally could not keep up with this phenomenal output, so at her death in 2000 she left behind an amazing 160 unpublished manuscripts, something that no other author has ever achieved.

Barbara's son, Ian McCorquodale, together with his daughter Iona, felt that it was their sacred duty to publish all these titles for Barbara's millions of admirers all over the world who so love her wonderful romances.

So in 2004 they started publishing the 160 brand new Barbara Cartlands as *The Barbara Cartland Pink Collection*, as Barbara's favourite colour was always pink – and yet more pink!

The Barbara Cartland Pink Collection is published monthly exclusively by Barbaracartland.com and the books are numbered in sequence from 1 to 160.

Enjoy receiving a brand new Barbara Cartland book each month by taking out an annual subscription to the Pink Collection, or purchase the books individually.

The Pink Collection is available from the Barbara Cartland website www.barbaracartland.com via mail order and through all good bookshops.

In addition Ian and Iona are proud to announce that The Barbara Cartland Pink Collection is now available in ebook format as from Valentine's Day 2011.

For more information, please contact us at:

Barbaracartland.com Ltd.
Camfield Place
Hatfield
Hertfordshire AL9 6JE
United Kingdom

Telephone: +44 (0)1707 642629
Fax: +44 (0)1707 663041
Email: info@barbaracartland.com

THE LATE DAME BARBARA CARTLAND

Barbara Cartland who sadly died in May 2000 at the age of nearly 99 was the world's most famous romantic novelist who wrote 723 books in her lifetime with worldwide sales of over 1 billion copies and her books were translated into 36 different languages.

As well as romantic novels, she wrote historical biographies, 6 autobiographies, theatrical plays, books of advice on life, love, vitamins and cookery. She also found time to be a political speaker and television and radio personality.

She wrote her first book at the age of 21 and this was called *Jigsaw*. It became an immediate bestseller and sold 100,000 copies in hardback and was translated into 6 different languages. She wrote continuously throughout her life, writing bestsellers for an astonishing 76 years. Her books have always been immensely popular in the United States, where in 1976 her current books were at numbers 1 & 2 in the B. Dalton bestsellers list, a feat never achieved before or since by any author.

Barbara Cartland became a legend in her own lifetime and will be best remembered for her wonderful romantic novels, so loved by her millions of readers throughout the world.

Her books will always be treasured for their moral message, her pure and innocent heroines, her good looking and dashing heroes and above all her belief that the power of love is more important than anything else in everyone's life.

"Much has been written about Royal marriages being arranged for political and dynastic convenience, but in my studies of history I have found many Royal marriages that have turned out to be real love matches however unlikely it might seem on the surface."

Barbara Cartland

CHAPTER ONE
1882

The Earl Granville, the British Secretary of State for Foreign Affairs, arrived at Windsor Castle not looking forward with any enthusiasm to his appointment with Her Majesty Queen Victoria.

As he was very popular with the equerries and other members of the Windsor Castle staff, he was greeted with obvious pleasure on his arrival.

He was politely offered something to drink after his journey from London.

The Earl refused and said that he could not stay too long as he had so much work to do at his office, but could he please see Her Majesty as quickly as possible.

An equerry hurried away and some twenty minutes later he returned to say,

"Her Majesty is in a good temper and so will be pleased to see you, my Lord."

"I am very glad to hear that," the Earl remarked, "because I am not sure when she does see me if she will be as pleased as she obviously is now."

Other members of the staff, who were listening to this conversation, laughed.

"She is always good-tempered with you, my Lord," one of them said. "It is when the Prime Minister comes that she is in a temper before he can even walk up the stairs!"

It was indeed well known to the Earl that the Queen disliked Mr. William Gladstone.

She had clashed violently with him in earlier years and at one time she had threatened to abdicate if he did not do what she wanted.

When Mr. Gladstone came back for a second term as Prime Minister, it had been only natural that those in attendance on Her Majesty were determined to keep him away from her as much as possible.

Unfortunately, as matters were becoming so tense in Europe and the Russians were behaving in what the Queen thought was a despicable manner, both the Prime Minister and his Secretary of State for Foreign Affairs, the Earl Granville, were practically daily visitors at Windsor Castle.

In fact when the Earl had said that he was visiting the Queen today, the equerry on duty had groaned almost noisily.

"I only hope, my Lord, that you don't bring Her Majesty bad news," he said, as he escorted the Earl up the stairs.

"I am afraid that Her Majesty will not be pleased at what I have to tell her," the Earl replied to him, "so you can prepare yourself for a fairly gloomy evening."

"We have those far too often," the equerry retorted. "If it is to do with the Russians again, I think we will bolt up the gates and refuse your Lordship and any of your staff admittance!"

The Earl laughed as he was meant to do.

At that moment they reached the passage that led to the Queen's Private Apartments.

"I will do my best not to make you as apprehensive as you are at the moment," the Earl said, as they walked towards another equerry standing expectantly at the far end of the corridor.

The Earl reached him.

He bowed and greeted the Earl,

"Good afternoon, my Lord, it is very good to see you again."

"Now that is the sort of greeting I like to have when I arrive," the Earl replied. "But they are full of gloom and doom downstairs and expect I will be about to upset Her Majesty and that will be the end of her good mood."

"I think I know why you have come," the equerry replied, "and all I can say, my Lord, is that you will be very lucky if you receive an elegant answer to the question you are going to put in front of Her Majesty."

"I am crossing my fingers and hoping for the best but expecting the worst," the Earl answered lightly.

The two equerries laughed as if they could not help themselves.

One of them opened the door and then ushered the Earl inside.

He returned almost immediately to say,

"Her Majesty is waiting to see you, my Lord."

He opened the door and the Earl went in.

The Queen, dressed in black mourning which she had worn ever since her beloved Prince Albert had died all of twenty years ago, was sitting near the window.

Sunshine was streaming in through the windows of the room and it seemed to envelope her.

The Earl, after bowing to her deeply, walked slowly towards her.

She appeared to be relaxed in a way that made her much less awe-inspiring than she usually was to those who visited her on affairs of State.

"Good morning, my Lord," she greeted the Earl. "I would be most pleased to see you if I could not guess why you have made this particular visit."

"As you know we are always sorry to do anything to upset Your Majesty," the Earl replied. "But, alas, there are many important matters that the Prime Minister and I cannot decide for ourselves."

He paused before he continued,

"Therefore we have to trouble Your Majesty even though we have no wish to do so."

The Queen smiled,

"I am always pleased to see you, my Lord, in any other capacity and I am always anxious to hear how your family is. So please let us get through the official business as quickly as possible."

The Earl gave a sigh of relief.

Her Majesty was indeed in an excellent humour as he had already seen and so perhaps things would not be as difficult as he expected they might be.

"What I have to tell Your Majesty," he began, "and, I know it has been said very often, is that another of the Principalities in the Balkan States is in desperate need of Your Majesty's help."

"I guessed that was why you had come," the Queen answered. "But I told you the last time you were here with the Prime Minister that I have no more relations to help the Principalities and they must look elsewhere for protection against those meddlesome Russians."

"If that were possible I am quite certain they would do as Your Majesty wishes," the Earl assured her. "But unfortunately the only country that the Russians have any fear of or at least any respect for is ours."

He knew as he spoke that it was impossible for the Queen to forget that it was entirely through her sending four Battleships through the Dardanelles that had halted the entire Russian Army when they were only within six miles of Constantinople.

Because they dared not fight against Great Britain, they had turned back in disarray.

As General Gorchakov had said at the time, it had cost them the lives of fifty thousand picked men and many millions of money for nothing.

After that Her Majesty was quite certain that they would not attempt to conquer Constantinople again or even make bellicose threats to Turkey.

But the Earl and the Prime Minister had discovered that they were still causing as much dissension and unrest in the smaller Principalities of the Balkans as they possibly could.

And the only way the Balkan Rulers could defend themselves was to take an English bride and fly the Union Jack to warn off the Russians or else the full might of the British Army and Navy would be thrown at them.

Queen Victoria was being called the 'Matchmaker of Europe' by everyone in diplomatic circles.

She had set many of her relations on thrones and saved them from invasion by the Russians and despite this the Russians themselves were behaving very badly.

They sent spies into the Principalities pretending to be salesmen of anything that country might want.

Once they were established they caused revolutions and uprisings, which had never happened before.

The Prince of every small Principality was terrified of a Russian invasion except when he was able to fly the Union Jack beside his own flag.

The Queen, who was violently against Russia, had taken a stand from the very beginning by proclaiming that she would help any Principality that she possibly could.

But unfortunately, as the Earl knew only too well, she had now run out of brides of Royal Blood, who were prepared to sit on a throne even though they knew from the beginning that it was very precarious.

Because the Queen was quick-witted and disliked wasting time when it was unnecessary, she said now and her voice sharpened,

"Who is asking for my help this time? I suppose I must listen to a tale of woe even though, as you know, my Lord, I am quite incapable of doing anything about it."

"That is exactly, Your Majesty," the Earl replied, "what the Prime Minister said to me only yesterday when unexpectedly we received a visit from Count Yuri Unkar from Samosia."

The Queen knitted her brow.

"Samosia?" she quizzed him. "Where is that?"

"It is quite a small Principality, ma'am," the Earl answered. "But, as Your Majesty will doubtless remember it is low down in the Balkans and nearer to the Aegean. It was where Your Majesty sent the British Battleships which successfully turned back the Russian Army."

"Of course I remember," the Queen answered him sharply. "But, as I have told you already, my Lord, I have no more brides for the Principalities and they must learn to fight for themselves."

There was silence for a moment and then the Earl said slowly,

"That is exactly what Mr. Gladstone said to me last night. But on thinking it over, because I am so sorry for the young Prince Ivor, who I happen to like very much, I suddenly remembered someone Your Majesty has clearly forgotten."

The Queen looked at him in surprise.

"Someone I have forgotten," she repeated. "But I have gone through all my relations and, of course, those of my dear husband most carefully. I really cannot find one more who would be ready to sacrifice herself to save a Balkan Prince."

"All the same, ma'am" the Earl said quietly, "it was nearly dawn when I suddenly thought of someone we had all forgotten."

The Queen looked at him again.

He knew that Her Majesty was intrigued and that she was waiting for him to say more.

He deliberately took his time before he spoke again,

"Of course Your Majesty was very young when it happened and I daresay if your mother spoke of it at all it was not in your presence."

"Who are you talking about?" the Queen asked him firmly.

At the same time the Earl realised that she was now very interested and in fact intrigued.

He therefore took his time before he continued,

"I am sure as a little girl nothing that could hurt or upset you was spoken of in your presence. Certainly not anything that caused a great deal of chatter and disapproval at the time."

Now the Queen was obviously thinking back into her childhood.

After what was almost a poignant silence she said,

"You have aroused my curiosity, my Lord, but I must admit that I cannot understand what you are trying to say."

"I am quite sure that Your Majesty has never given a thought to it since you became Queen," the Earl went on. "But then the older members of Your Majesty's family will surely recall the tremendous commotion and upset there was when your cousin, a handsome young man of twenty-seven, married beneath him and was then, to all intents and purposes, thrown out of the family."

Her Majesty drew in her breath.

Then she gave a little cry.

"Now I know who you are talking about. It is my cousin Prince Vladimir of Leiningen you are talking about, is it not?"

"I am indeed, ma'am," he confirmed, "and while Your Majesty has not seen Prince Vladimir since he left the family in disgrace, I can tell you that he is a very happy man and his marriage has been a very successful one."

The Queen looked at him as if she could hardly believe what he was saying.

Then, in a very different voice from the one she had used previously, she said scathingly,

"To an actress, to a woman who performs in public, that is impossible!"

"Sometimes in life, ma'am," the Earl replied, "the impossible becomes the possible. In this case I have never known a man as happy as Prince Vladimir. I know that neither he nor his wife have ever regretted that they were brave enough to snub Society and be married despite the fact that they would be isolated."

"You say that the marriage has been a success?" the Queen asked curiously.

"A complete and absolute success. If Your Majesty would look back and perhaps talk to someone who was alive at the time, you will remember that Prince Vladimir's wife was *not*, as was presumed at the time, a common girl, who wished to portray herself on the stage merely because she was pretty enough to please the men watching her."

The Earl paused.

Then, as the Queen did not speak, he carried on,

"She was a brilliant pianist. Because the music she composed pleased so many people, she was invited to play her own music in the theatre and, perhaps unfortunately, her piece was included in one of the most successful and the most talked about shows that took place in London at the time."

"It should have been impossible," the Queen said with disapproval in her voice, "for a Prince of the Royal Blood to marry such a woman."

"That is just what your mother and a great number of other people said," he replied. "But they did marry and they left London and, as far as I know, have never been back since."

"Then where are they now?" the Queen enquired as if she could not help being curious.

"They have been living quietly in Devon," the Earl told her. "As far as I can make out, they have never been anywhere near London since they left all those years ago immediately after their marriage."

"In Devon!" the Queen exclaimed. "How did you meet them, my Lord?"

"On a brief holiday I took recently, when I stopped my yacht not far from Plymouth."

The Earl could see how intrigued the Queen was and he continued,

"As I stepped ashore, I saw a man with a very pretty girl beside him. He was about to board a small ship that had just come into Port. After I had taken a second glance at him, I realised to my surprise that the man was Prince Vladimir himself."

The Queen did not interrupt him and the Earl went on,

"He was just as handsome as he had been when we were at Oxford together. He had still kept that youthful air which made one feel that everything that happened to him was exciting. He certainly appeared to be delighted to see me and we reminisced for quite a while about our time at University together."

"I understood at the time that he had disappeared completely," the Queen said, "and no one knew where he was."

"That is true, ma'am," the Earl confirmed. "A great many people thought that he had gone abroad. As they said, it was the right place for him after marrying beneath himself in such a disgraceful manner."

He hesitated and then the Queen asked,

"But they were mistaken?"

"Very much mistaken as it happens, ma'am. They are, although it may be difficult to believe it, still blissfully happy and still thrilled with each other. In fact it would be somewhat difficult for me to say that I have ever seen two people happier than they are."

"How extraordinary!" the Queen exclaimed.

"Of course now Prince Vladimir has a family, the eldest being a very beautiful girl called Linetta."

There was silence and then the Queen enquired,

"Does my cousin still call himself *Prince*?"

"They live in a very small village in the centre of Devon," the Earl explained. "I think the people there know all about him and admire him as much as he was admired when he was one of the smartest and most popular young gentlemen in London."

There was a short pause before the Queen asked, as if she could not help herself,

"And his wife?"

"His wife is still very beautiful and I believe is still playing the piano brilliantly as she did in the theatre."

The Queen coughed and commented,

"I cannot really believe what you are suggesting, my Lord,"

The Earl smiled.

"I knew that Your Majesty would guess without my telling you why we are talking about your cousin."

"How old is the girl?" the Queen demanded.

"Linetta is twenty on her next birthday and not only as beautiful as her mother, but if I am to believe her father, she is just as talented."

"So she plays the piano too," the Queen retorted. "Is she going on the stage as well – ?"

"Most certainly *not*, ma'am," the Earl replied and there was a sharpness to his voice.

He composed himself a little before he went on,

"Prince Vladimir has very decided ideas about his family. The boys, I understand, have gone to Eton, but are not using their title because it might prejudice people at the school in one way or another to treat them differently to the other boys."

"And the girl?" the Queen asked.

"Linetta, I understand, is called Lady Linetta by the village people simply because her father's friends call her that to save any embarrassment."

"And my cousin himself?" the Queen enquired as if it was an effort to do so.

"He explained to me that he thought it would be a big mistake to be a Prince, especially as he had no wish for

11

people to know the trouble he had caused in his family. So he merely calls himself Baron, which naturally is quite true as he is one as well as being a Prince."

"And his wife has been content with all this?" the Queen asked as if it did not seem possible.

"She is content with anything as long as it makes him happy. That is why I can say quite honestly to Your Majesty that they are indeed the happiest couple that I have ever met and as much in love now as when they ran away together."

He was thinking as he spoke of the commotion the scandal had caused in the Royal family at the time.

And how the newspapers had tried so hard to find out where they had gone and failed.

Because Prince Vladimir had been so well known in the London Social world and continually written about in the Court columns, the idea of him running away with a girl in the theatre was, of course, a major sensation at the time and the gossips had a field day.

It was the sort of news that was reported in detail in every newspaper at the time.

Now, like so much in life, all the excitement had gradually died away.

Prince Vladimir and his beautiful actress wife, once they had vanished from London, were eventually forgotten and no one asked about them again.

As if the Queen knew just what he was thinking, she remarked,

"And they were certainly extremely clever at hiding themselves away. They were even forgotten by my own family."

"But now I have found them." the Earl replied. "It seems to me, ma'am, that Linetta is the perfect prospect for

Your Majesty to now suggest as a bride for Prince Ivor of Samosia."

He paused before he went on,

"After all she is a Princess by birth. I just cannot imagine that a stigma of any sort will be an obstacle after all these years have passed by when her father and mother have been out of sight and out of mind."

He gave a little laugh before he added,

"Even I was rather surprised to see them alive. I felt almost apologetic for not having realised before how cleverly they had hidden themselves away and so had been forgotten by the *Beau Monde*."

There was a long silence before the Queen quizzed the Earl again,

"Are you quite sure, my Lord, that there is no one else?"

"No one knows better than Your Majesty," the Earl told her, "that we have used up every one of your other relations and everybody in England who has enough Royal blood to intimidate the Russians."

Again there was a silence until the Queen said,

"I think the only possible way that this girl could be offered to Prince Ivor is that she goes to Samosia without anyone in England knowing what is happening until the marriage can be announced as a *fait accompli*."

"I agree with Your Majesty," the Earl answered. "That would make things very much easier for her and for Your Majesty to offer her to Prince Ivor."

He looked thoughtful before he carried on,

"To revive the old story of Prince Vladimir's elopement now would undoubtedly appear in the English newspapers and copied by the Press in the Balkans and perhaps even in Russia as well."

"Have you talked this possibility over with Prince Ivor?" the Queen asked him.

The Earl shook his head.

"The idea only occurred to me a few days ago when the Secretary of State for Samosia arrived at 10 Downing Street only to be told positively and truthfully that Your Majesty could not do any more than you have done already for the Balkan States."

"So you have not spoken of this to anyone else?" the Queen wanted to know.

"No one at all, ma'am, and not even to her father, Prince Vladimir."

The Queen looked surprised.

"You mean you did not suggest it when you were in Devon with them?" she asked incredulously.

"Of course not, ma'am. I did not worry myself at that time with thinking about our own troubles. I was on holiday and it was delightful to meet an old friend I had not seen for so long."

He smiled as he continued,

"We talked of Eton where we had been together, and Oxford where the Prince had distinguished himself at cricket, which endeared him to everyone in the University. We were great friends there as young men. We were both in the second eleven and always hoped that we would be promoted into the first!"

The Queen laughed as if she could not help it.

"I have always tried to understand that the game of cricket is far more important than anything else in your lives!"

"Of course it is," the Earl agreed. "But now, as Secretary of State for Foreign Affairs, I have to beg Your Majesty and Prince Vladimir if he agrees to save one more

Principality from the dastardly Russians who needless to say are using their clever tricks to incite violence amongst the ordinary people and creating a situation when it will be impossible to stop them forcing their way into the country and taking it over."

"The Russians are really behaving appallingly!" the Queen exclaimed.

"I do agree with you, ma'am. The only person who has been able to protect the Balkans against them is Your Majesty."

There was a long pause before the Earl said,

"I could not help thinking it was almost a gift from Heaven when I came back to London to find the Prime Minister absolutely certain there was nothing we could do to help Prince Ivor and saying to everyone who suggested it that it was useless to bother Your Majesty for yet another relation."

The Earl knew well as he was speaking that he was playing a difficult and subtle card.

He recognised that the Queen had a strong dislike of Mr. Gladstone.

She had raged at him on more than one occasion and it would obviously be a pleasure for her to show him once again that he was wrong.

The Earl waited expectantly as he saw that the idea was passing through her mind.

At the same time he was well aware that she was remembering how angry her family had been when Prince Vladimir had fallen in love and had thought that nothing else in the world was of any consequence.

'He was right,' the Earl told himself. 'But it would be a great triumph for matters of the heart if the daughter of a man who gave up everything that had been important to him for love should become, to all intents and purposes, a Queen.'

There was a long silence.

Yet it now seemed to the Earl as if the sunshine was deepening and becoming more brilliant than it had been when he entered the room.

When at last the Queen spoke, it seemed to the Earl as if he had waited an eternity for her to do so.

"What I suggest, my Lord," she said slowly, "is that you go back to Plymouth where you found your friend and tell him that, if his daughter wishes to become the bride of Prince Ivor, I will then give her my blessing and protection and she may proceed to Samosia as soon as it is possible to arrange suitable transport for her."

It was with an effort that the Earl prevented himself from cheering.

As it was, he merely bowed a little lower than usual as he said,

"Your Majesty is most gracious and understanding. I know in saving the people of Samosia from being overrun by the Russians that Your Majesty will have the gratitude of every person in that country and throughout the Balkans as well."

"I have one thing to add to what I have already said and it is very important," the Queen declared.

The Earl waited, hoping that she had not changed her mind.

Then she said firmly,

"No one is to know, my Lord, that I have given you my permission to go to Plymouth to see Prince Vladimir and to discuss this delicate matter with him."

She stopped for a moment before she went on,

"It would be a great mistake if, by any chance, the Prince does not wish his daughter to undertake such a task and the newspapers then learn that we were obliged to tell Samosia that we could not assist them in any way."

The Earl bowed.

"I understand, ma'am, and I think it is a very wise and sensible thing to do. And you can, of course, trust me implicitly. So I will take a little time off from my work to travel to Plymouth and will then be able to bring you back the answer."

"As you have already told me that speed is of the essence, I will let you proceed at once," the Queen said. "I will be hoping to hear from you in four or five days, my Lord."

The Earl realised that she was working out in her mind how long it would take him to reach Devon.

He thought that the quickest way would be to go by train.

However, he did not say this as it was not pertinent how he travelled to Devon so long as he did.

Instead he bowed once again as he said,

"I can only thank Your Majesty for being so very understanding and to realise the importance of keeping the Russians firmly in their own country and well away from the Balkans."

"It is something they have no intention of doing," the Queen replied, "but that is what you have to make the Prime Minister understand, although I would admit that it is a hard task."

Her voice changed noticeably now that she was speaking about Mr. Gladstone.

Because the Earl knew how much she disliked him, he said quickly,

"I can only thank Your Majesty from the bottom of my heart for being so understanding. I hope to return with good news as quickly as possible."

The Queen held out her hand and he bent over it.

Then he moved slowly backwards to the door.

As he reached it, it was opened and he went out.

The same equerry was waiting outside and said as the Earl reappeared,

"You have been quite a long time, my Lord. I was hoping that things were going smoothly."

"Very smoothly indeed," the Earl relied. "In fact I have left you nothing to worry about, which I know is to your satisfaction."

"It certainly is, my Lord. Would you like some tea or a glass of champagne before you leave us?"

"Unfortunately I will now have to return to London immediately," the Earl answered, "as I have a meeting this evening. But many thanks for your offer and on another occasion we will then propose the health of Great Britain's success in everything she may undertake."

"I will certainly drink to that," the equerry laughed.

They reached the ground floor and walked to the front door where the carriage that had brought the Earl to Windsor Castle was waiting.

He thanked the equerry for looking after him and shook him by the hand.

Climbing into the carriage, he told the driver to go back to London as quickly as was possible.

As they turned out of the gates of Windsor Castle, the Earl was thinking with satisfaction he had brought off what he might well consider a complete triumph.

The one difficulty would be, he thought, to kerb the Prime Minister's tongue and he therefore decided to say as little as possible to him.

Equally he realised that the Secretary of State for Foreign Affairs for Samosia, Count Yuri Unkar, would be waiting for him at his office.

He was a very well-spoken man to whom the Earl had felt friendly from the first moment they had met.

He had been most polite and apologetic in asking for England's help.

But, as he had said, it was the only chance they had of saving themselves from the greed and ambition of the Russians in expanding their already enormous Empire and to seize as much power as possible in Europe and to extend their reach to the Mediterranean.

And most of all to save Samosia, which was a large and prosperous country, would be a triumph for Britain and surely prove to be another disaster and disappointment for the Czar.

From all accounts Czar Alexander III was a very unpleasant man who was already generally disliked by his own people.

He was absolutely determined to gain more land in the Balkans for Russia.

At the same time the Earl suspected that his mind was on a very different matter.

In fact it was being whispered that the Russians desired eventually to conquer India and take it away from the British Empire.

Many Cossacks were already rampaging over Asia and doing a great deal of harm to the small local tribes.

They were, he had been informed secretly, creeping nearer and nearer to India every day.

They were using their increasing power and their fast horses to ensure that a great many places in Asia were now under Russian rule.

The Earl sighed as he thought that India would have to defend herself very much more than she was doing at the moment and, if she did not, the Russians would obtain a victory that would be a bitter blow to the Union Jack and Great Britain's influence in the world.

When he arrived back in London, the Earl learnt at the War Office that the Prime Minister had received an urgent message to visit someone of great consequence who lived in Norfolk.

As this was the opposite direction from where he would be going the next morning, the Earl thought that he had every reason to be delighted that the Prime Minister was not there to question him.

Telling a junior official that he had been called away on important family business and would not be able to communicate with the Prime Minister until he returned, the Earl made it clear that he had nothing special to say about the afternoon's visit to Her Majesty the Queen at Windsor Castle.

He then went straight to his own office where, as he had expected, he found the Secretary of State for Samosia waiting for him.

Count Yuri Unkar was a very good-looking man of fifty and he was sitting comfortably in an armchair when the Earl entered the room.

He sprang up and exclaimed,

"You are back, my Lord, and I am sure that you have something exciting to tell me."

"I will tell you everything word for word," the Earl replied. "But as we have to leave first thing in the morning for Plymouth, I will now have to return to my home and tell my wife where I am going."

He smiled before he added,

"She will not be particularly pleased I am leaving as we have a party tomorrow night at which unfortunately only my wife will now be present. You and I will also miss the weekend amusements we had planned for you at our house in the country."

"You are so very kind and hospitable," the Count answered, "but I am intrigued to know where we are going and why?"

"That is a complete and absolute secret," the Earl answered. "But I will tell you all I am allowed to do when we set forth soon after dawn. We are travelling by train so I suggest that you meet me at my office in three hours' time."

"You mean that we are leaving tonight!" the Count exclaimed in surprise.

"Well, actually very early tomorrow morning," the Earl told him. "But it will be so much more comfortable if we spend the night sleeping in our own beds, so we will not leave until after breakfast."

"I see your point," the Count replied. "I understand that we must not waste any time."

"None at all and, if you come with me now, I will take you in my carriage and drop you off where you are staying before I go home."

"I am most grateful," the Count said, "and I am positive that I will be more grateful than I can possibly say when we have achieved our objective."

He paused before he continued,

"I can only guess that Her Majesty is behind us and approves of what we are doing."

It was a question more than a statement, as the Earl realised.

Then, because he thought it would be a mistake to talk too much or to excite the Count unnecessarily until the future was more or less foolproof, he merely said,

"We must make haste."

As he spoke, he turned away to give instructions to his assistant of where he was going in the morning and to reserve two First Class tickets for him on the early train to Plymouth.

CHAPTER TWO

Actually it was after nine o'clock the next morning when they arrived at Paddington Station to catch the train that the Earl had been informed departed promptly at half-past-nine.

It would mean two changes before they could reach Plymouth.

He had also, when he had bid goodbye to the Count last night, told him to make sure that the ship he had come in from the Balkans proceeded at once to Plymouth to dock there and await instructions.

He was certain that this would take some time.

But if they were successful in the mission they were undertaking, the Count would be able to return to Samosia with the good news, or even better still, with the bride-to-be herself.

'I hope I have thought of everything,' the Earl said to himself when he woke up early in the morning.

He asked himself the same question when he had finished breakfast and his wife wanted to know when he would be returning.

"As soon as I can, dearest," he replied. "But you know what people are like. It is so often impossible for them to make up their minds as quickly as you have always done."

His wife laughed and kissed him.

"Take care of yourself," she said, "and I will try to keep the wolves from the door while you are away. But you know as well as I do that the moment you have left there will be half-a-dozen people turning up wanting to see you to solve their problems for them."

The Earl smiled.

"It is one of the penalties of working with foreign countries," he said. "At the same time I find it extremely interesting."

"I know you do," she answered, "but I am jealous as they take up much more of your time than you reserve for me!"

"I will try to behave better when I return," the Earl grinned and kissed his wife again.

They were very happily married.

He often thought how lucky he was to have a wife who understood the difficulties of his appointment and she very seldom complained that he was neglecting her.

The Earl and the Count had then been driven to Paddington Station.

They found that the Earl's Secretary had reserved a comfortable First Class carriage for them and had informed the restaurant car that they required a table in a quiet part of the carriage.

This was always essential when the Earl travelled just in case anyone should overhear what he was saying.

There were, as he well knew, inevitably spies from different countries who were told to watch the Secretary of State for Foreign Affairs in particular.

And he was always fully aware that a remark made casually might prove disastrous to his country.

Thus security was of the utmost importance for all members of the Government.

The Earl's valet, who was travelling with them, had procured all the morning newspapers.

He had brought a bottle of the Earl's champagne to be put on ice in the restaurant car so that they could send for it at any time.

"You certainly travel in comfort," the Count said as the train started to move off. "The trains to Constantinople are already passing through the Balkans on the main lines, but we who live some distance from Sofia find it difficult to travel in any way, except as we always have, behind our horses."

"I cannot say that I really like trains," the Earl told him. "I am glad that you have told your ship to proceed immediately to Plymouth."

"I sent my instructions to the Captain first thing this morning, my Lord. As he is a good sailor, who has been at sea for many years, I am sure that he will have no difficulty in finding his way there."

The Earl had considered the idea of them travelling to Plymouth in the ship belonging to Samosia.

But as time was what really mattered, there would be nothing quicker than going there by train.

The one they were in was certainly as up to date as he had expected and he was convinced that there would be no quicker way of reaching Prince Vladimir and his house in Devon.

The train itself was actually faster than the Earl had hoped, even though there were numerous stops at which he felt that precious time was wasted.

It was getting dark when finally, after what seemed to him long hours of boredom, the train finally puffed its way into the Station at Plymouth.

"We have actually arrived!" the Count exclaimed excitedly.

It was with difficulty that the Earl did not say how glad he was that the journey was now over.

He always found it most difficult to sleep in a train unless he could lie down fully.

This he was unable to do in their reserved carriage as there were no arrangements for sleepers and nor were the carriages convertible as they were just beginning to be on the expresses heading to Scotland.

The Earl managed to shut his eyes and made it clear to the Count that he wished to rest rather than talk.

The Count found himself gazing out of the carriage window at the green fields and the attractive countryside they were passing through.

He hoped that the journey would not take long and that his expectations would not turn out to be as difficult as he anticipated they might be on their arrival.

A messenger had, in fact, been sent from the Earl's office. He had travelled all night and would, the Earl had reckoned, reach Plymouth at midday.

Prince Vladimir would therefore be aware of their arrival several hours before their train reached Plymouth and would not be put out if they had arrived at his house suddenly and unannounced.

'I only hope,' the Earl said to himself, 'that he will meet us at the station.'

It was only because the Count had been so eloquent in explaining the terrible situation they were in in Samosia that had made him realise that it would be cruelty to delay matters any more than was absolutely necessary.

In fact, the Earl thought, as the train drew to a halt that he could not imagine any Government Department, except his own, moving so quickly.

The Earl knew that, if the Russians were causing trouble in Samosia, it would be very cruel as well as being disastrous to deny them the help he hoped and prayed that he would be able to offer them.

To his great relief there was a carriage waiting at the Station.

As soon as the footman found out who they were, their luggage, that had been supervised by the Earl's valet, was hurriedly taken to a porter.

As they finally drove away from Plymouth Station, the Earl gave a deep sigh of relief.

There was always a distinct possibility that Prince Vladimir might have been away from his home, in which case their journey would have been a complete waste of time.

Or he might have been reluctant to receive visitors thrust upon him unexpectedly.

The Earl, however, always found that the average person extended a deep respect for those who served their country in the Cabinet.

He had learnt that a call from the Prime Minister or any of his colleagues was in itself as vital as a summons from Windsor Castle.

"Well, we are here," the Earl said, as the closed carriage drawn by two well matched horses set off at a brisk pace.

"I think you are really splendid, my Lord, in how swiftly you have arranged everything," the Count told him. "I only wish that we could be as effective in Samosia as you are in England."

"I should have thought the difficulties you suffer at the moment of never knowing what will happen the next day or the day after that," the Earl remarked, "is something that invariably must keep you alert and on your toes."

"We are certainly very scared," the Count admitted. "But it was only in the last two or three months that we have realised just how much the Russians were infiltrating upon us and how cleverly they have talked a small number of people into being aggressive and causing trouble in the towns and villages."

The Earl, who had heard this story before in other Principalities, knew exactly how astute the Russians were in infiltrating into a country and urging the people to rebel against their Rulers.

As the horses left the town of Plymouth, the roads were fairly smooth and they enjoyed the peace and quiet of the Devon countryside.

The Earl thought how fortunate the English were to have no fears of an invasion or of infiltration by foreigners, who wished to conquer their beloved country and enslave their people.

He could easily understand how nerve-wracking it must be to be never quite certain when one woke up if the people were in revolt.

Or if the Russians were moving across the border to take over villages and towns before the inhabitants had any idea of what was happening,

'I must help this man as much as I can,' the Earl thought to himself.

And he knew that it was only a question of time.

Once the Russians had taken hold of the country and deprived Prince Ivor of his throne, it would be almost impossible for anyone to do anything about it.

He just hoped that Prince Vladimir, who he recalled now called himself a Baron, would not prevaricate or waste time unnecessarily.

Prince Vladimir's house was only ten miles from Plymouth.

After passing through numerous cornfields and then a large wood, they came in sight of a most attractive Manor

House nestling in a pretty green valley not far from a small village.

As they drove up a long drive with silver birch trees on either side of it, the Earl could see in front of them a delightful country house.

Its windows were glittering in the sunshine and just in front of it was a stream running under a bridge towards a small lake.

The carriage came to a standstill outside the front door, which was reached by several steps.

A footman in a very smart livery was in the process of laying a red carpet down them.

As the Earl climbed out of the carriage and walked up the steps followed by the Count, a butler with grey hair bowed politely.

"His Lordship is waiting for you, my Lord," he informed the Earl, "but he did not expect you to arrive so quickly from the Station."

"We did not waste any time," the Earl replied, "and surprisingly our train was not late."

The butler smiled.

"You can never depend on them trains, my Lord," he answered. "Some guests we were expecting last week were three hours late as there had been a breakdown on the line."

As the butler finished speaking, he opened the door in front of him and announced,

"The Earl Granville, my Lord, and a companion."

The Earl had deliberately not given the butler the name of the Count.

He had merely said that he was bringing a friend and would explain why when he arrived.

As he entered the room, he noticed that many vases of brightly coloured flowers filled the air with a delicious fragrance.

Sunshine was streaming into the room through a French window that led into the garden where there was a large fountain playing.

For a moment the glitter seemed to blind the Earl's eyes.

It was only seconds later that he realised that Prince Vladimir was standing in front of him and holding out his hand.

At forty-six years of age he was still as handsome as he had been before he left London for ever and it was not difficult to understand why he had been so popular with the *Beau Monde* of the time.

It was always said that every *debutante* hoped that he would look in her direction and ask her to dance.

"Welcome, my Lord," Prince Vladimir was saying. "This is a very unexpected visit."

"It is so very good to see you again," the Earl said. "And I have often wondered if you would ever return to London."

"I am perfectly happy where I am," Prince Vladimir answered. "As you know, I have been away for so long I would hardly know my way down Piccadilly!"

The Earl laughed.

"I am sure that is not true," he retorted. "If you did come back, there would be many willing hands to show you around again."

"Fortunately I have no intention of returning," he answered. "But, please do sit down and I expect after that tiring journey, which I am very glad to say that I do not have to undertake, you would welcome a drink."

"We would certainly not refuse one," the Earl said. "Now let me introduce you to someone I have brought with me who is the reason for my visit to you."

He introduced the Count.

He was well aware that, as Prince Vladimir shook his hand, he was looking at him curiously.

The Earl thought with a feeling of concern that it was somewhat suspiciously.

As if the butler knew what was expected of him, he entered at that moment with a tray on which there was a bottle of champagne.

There were also a number of *petits-fours* on a silver salver.

The drinks were handed round and, when the butler had left the room, Prince Vladimir said,

"Now let's get down to business. I do realise that you have come here in a hurry and so I don't wish to waste your time or mine."

"That is true," the Earl murmured. "To waste time would, as I am sure you are well aware, give the Russians an advantage they would not ignore."

"The Russians?"

Prince Vladimir repeated the words just beneath his breath.

At the same time there was a question in his eyes that told the Earl he was now suspicious as to why they were there.

"I think, Your Royal Highness – " the Earl began.

Prince Vladimir held up his hand.

"Wait a moment," he said. "I think you are aware that here I am a mere Baron which I called myself when I left London. Most of my servants here have no idea that I have any other title."

"I am sorry," the Earl apologised. "I will not make the same mistake again. Equally it is difficult for me not to remember you as you were when you used to come and stay with me and play in the cricket matches we arranged every year."

Prince Vladimir smiled.

"That is true and, of course, I have not forgotten. At that time you called me by my Christian name and that is how it should be now."

The Earl chuckled.

"Very well, Vladimir, and may I say that you have altered very little during the years."

"Thank you indeed, George," he answered. "Now you must tell me please why you are here."

"That is just what I was about to do," the Earl said. "I hope you will understand without my going into details the menace the Russians currently are to Bulgaria and other Balkan States. Therefore I think you will guess why the Secretary of State for Foreign Affairs, Count Yuri Unkar, is with me."

He saw Prince Vladimir stiffen.

He knew, because he had always been very quick-brained, that he had already guessed why he and the Count were now sitting opposite him.

And the Earl thought that it was only right for him to put his project clearly in front of Prince Vladimir, so he stated firmly,

"Samosia, where my friend the Count is Secretary of State for Foreign Affairs, is now on the verge of being invaded by the Russians."

He hesitated before he further explained,

"His country, as I am sure you know, is very close to the sea and the Russians need, above all, an exit into the Aegean that will lead them into the Mediterranean."

The Earl could very easily see by the expression on Prince Vladimir's face that he was well aware of this and went on,

"Her Majesty Queen Victoria, has, as I am sure you know, sent a good number of her relatives as brides to the Principalities of the Balkans. She is rightly now known as 'The Matchmaker of Europe'."

"Yes, yes," Prince Vladimir said hurriedly. "Please go on."

"Well, now another Prince has begged for her help and, as she has no more relatives, she thought that she must refuse him his request point-blank and let Samosia suffer."

There was a long silence as the Earl finished.

Then at last, as if the tension was too much for him, the Count spoke up,

"Please, please, Your Royal Highness, if you do not help us the Russians will move in and I expect as happened in so many Principalities that they will kill the Prince and his family and take over the whole country."

There was another poignant silence.

Then Prince Vladimir said looking at the Earl rather than at the Count,

"I knew when your messenger said that you were accompanied by a Samosian that there was a reason why you were seeking me out after all these years when I had thought that everyone had forgotten me."

"You are still a cousin of Her Majesty the Queen", the Earl declared quietly.

"And I would suppose that makes you think I will give you my daughter and send her into danger in a country that most people have never even heard of."

"She will be in no danger, as you well know," the Earl assured him, "if she has the blessing of the Queen of

Great Britain and proudly carries with her the Union Jack and the protection of the British Army and Navy."

Prince Vladimir rose and walked across the room to the French window.

He stood gazing at the fountain throwing its water up towards the sky, so that every drop of it glittered in the sunshine.

Then he said without turning round,

"I have been so happy here with my family and I know that they have been completely happy with me."

He hesitated before he continued,

"Why on earth should I ruin everything by letting my daughter go to a foreign land I have never visited to marry a foreigner I have never even seen?"

"I understand your feelings," the Earl said. "At the same time Her Majesty the Queen has no one else who she can send. Prince Ivor and all the people of Samosia are on their knees begging us for help."

Then the Count spoke up again,

"If Your Royal Highness will not let your daughter save us, then I think you must face the fact that hundreds, if not thousands, of our people will die and it is unlikely that the Prince of Samosia and any of his relations will stay alive."

Prince Vladimir did not answer.

Then the Earl rose from his chair and walked to stand beside him at the window.

"I know it is very difficult, Vladimir," he said, "for you to face such a problem."

He smiled at him before he continued,

"I promise you that I would not have suggested it if I had not felt it wrong for England to let the Russians take over a country that could in consequence be a grave danger to our own people as well as to those countries bordering the Mediterranean."

Prince Vladimir did not respond and the Earl went on,

"Her Majesty's first impulse was to affirm that she could do nothing. In fact she had forgotten that you were her cousin. As the years have passed by – twenty-two of them if I am not mistaken – a great number of people have forgotten you too."

"That is just what I hoped they would do," Prince Vladimir said.

"But there are many others just like myself," the Earl continued, "who remember you as you were and have regretted that you were still not with us."

The Earl spoke very quietly.

Yet he realised that Prince Vladimir was becoming wary of his persuasive arguments.

Again there was silence until Prince Vladimir said,

"You are asking too much. How can I possibly part with my daughter?"

It was a difficult question to answer and the Earl said,

"If she is as beautiful as I would expect a child of yours to be, then sooner or later she will be married and leave you. If she goes to Samosia, there is no reason at all why you should not visit her there regularly."

He smiled as he went on,

"After all, Vladimir, the turmoil you caused when you married has never reached Samosia and then you can expect a lot of people in London to have also forgotten you."

Prince Vladimir laughed.

"I might well have remembered," he said, "that you always had an answer to every question, George. I think you are a very clever man and I can understand why you are where you are now."

"That is easily the nicest compliment I have had for years!"

The Earl looked serious as he continued,

"I realise, Vladimir, that this is a terrible problem for you, but then for your daughter it is a chance of making herself not only the saviour of Samosia but, because she is your daughter, she could make it one of the most famous and respected countries in the whole of the Balkans and even of Europe too."

Prince Vladimir then let out a deep sigh and there was silence for what seemed to the Earl a very long time.

Then he suggested,

"I tell you what we must now do. You must talk to Linetta. She must be the one to decide her own future. If you are persuasive enough, you could be able to make her realise that this is an opportunity for her to save the lives of thousands of people or just pass by on the other side."

The Earl and the Count were listening intently and he went on,

"Then it is up to her, not to me, to say 'yes' or 'no' to your proposition, George."

Without waiting for the Earl's reply, he turned and walked to the mantelpiece and pulled on the bell-rope that hung beside it.

As if he felt that he needed sustenance, he walked over to where the butler had put the champagne and poured himself another full glass before he then offered it to his guests.

Both men refused as they still had some left in their glasses beside them.

The door opened and the butler appeared.

"Please will you ask Lady Linetta to come to me here, Hunter," Prince Vladimir ordered.

"Very good, my Lord," Hunter replied.

He closed the door and the Earl said,

"I am very sorry, Vladimir, to have upset you. But I promise you that there is no one else in the whole of the country we could turn to for help."

There was silence for a moment.

"In fact," he continued, "we have been through Her Majesty's relations and most of my assistants too had completely forgotten that you existed."

"I presume you were the only one who remembered it," Prince Vladimir said sourly.

"It would be impossible for me to forget you when we were such friends," the Earl replied.

Prince Vladimir gave another sigh,

"We have indeed had some happy times together in the past, George."

"And I would like to have more of them now," the Earl answered. "But then you hid yourself away very cleverly. It was only a year ago that I happened by chance to learn where you were."

"I am glad I was bright enough to cover my tracks," Prince Vladimir retorted.

The Earl was about to answer him when the door opened and a girl came in.

As she walked across the room, the Earl turned to look at her.

He was wondering if after all this she would be a disappointment.

Then, as she came towards him and he looked at her critically, he realised that she was in every way exactly what he had hoped she would be.

37

He recalled that her mother had been acclaimed as beautiful and her father had always been outstandingly handsome.

It was not surprising therefore that she was lovely in a very different way from any woman he had ever seen before. In fact there as only one word to describe her and that was 'ethereal'.

Her hair was fair with an occasional touch of red in it.

Her eyes were the blue of the Mediterranean and were framed with dark eyelashes.

He somehow expected her to be like so many of the English aristocracy, which was to be pretty, but without the outstanding features that would make her different from her contemporaries.

As the Earl had been aware, Linetta was twenty.

Being a tall girl with an exquisite figure she walked elegantly across the room.

Not, as was expected of an English *debutante*, but with a grace that somehow made her appear exceptional and enchanting at the same time.

She was so completely different from other women in a way that he could not explain.

As she drew nearer, the Earl realised that she was lovely in an individual manner of her own.

Her skin was perfect and her face was dominated by the largeness and the unique beauty of her eyes.

Her neck was long and this made her seem taller than she actually was.

'She would make a perfect Queen,' he thought to himself.

He knew that if she sat on a throne everyone seeing her would find it just impossible to look away or to notice anyone else.

As Linetta reached the Earl, she looked up at him and smiled saying,

"Papa was astonished when he was told that you were coming here today, my Lord. But I have always wanted to meet you because he has so often talked about the exciting games of cricket you arranged at your house and he said that you were undoubtedly the best bowler in the team."

"That is certainly true," the Earl answered. "May I say he has been greatly missed, but I hope your brother is as good at cricket as your father."

"He is in the First Eleven at Eton," Linetta said proudly. "But, of course, he will be leaving Eton next year and going to Oxford, where he hopes he will be chosen to play in the University Eleven."

"If he is anything like his father he most surely will be," the Earl replied.

"I must tell him that, my Lord. I know it will make him very keen to go to Oxford. At the same time he is not sure if he would not rather go to a French University than an English one or even go to Italy to study art in Florence or Rome."

Linetta glanced at her father as she spoke.

Prince Vladimir turned to the Count and said,

"You see I have difficulties even in my own family. If I am allowed to choose, I would want Charles to go to Oxford."

"Where you yourself excelled at cricket," the Earl intercepted, "and I enjoyed rowing with you in the boat races more than I have ever enjoyed any sport."

The two men laughed.

Then unexpectedly Linetta asked,

"But why are you gentlemen here if it is not an impertinent question? Why was Papa so upset when your messanger arrived early this morning to tell us that you were coming to see him?"

She moved towards at her father.

Then, as he looked almost appealingly at his friend, the Earl suggested,

"Please sit down, Lady Linetta, and let me tell you that my friend and I have come here especially to see you."

"To see *me*!" Linetta cried in astonishment. "Why should you want to see me?"

The Earl thought that many men would be able to answer that question quite simply.

But aloud he said,

"We have a most important proposition to put in front of you. I hope that you will listen to it and study it in the same way as your father studied at Oxford and, as you doubtless know, won First Class Honours, which he had worked very hard to achieve."

"Is it as bad as all that?" Linetta asked.

Then, as if she was curious, she looked at the Count who she had not been introduced to.

The Earl followed the direction of her eyes and then quickly added,

"I am sorry that I am so remiss as not to introduce you to my friend, Count Yuri Unkar, who is the Secretary of State for Foreign Affairs in Samosia, a large country in the Balkans."

He thought, as Linetta put out her hand towards the Count, that there was an expression in her eyes that had not been there before.

The Earl was certain that she was shrewd enough now to be aware that the reason for their visit definitely concerned her and her future.

CHAPTER THREE

There was rather an uncomfortable pause and then the Earl addressed the Count,

"I think, Yuri, this is where you say your piece."

He realised as he spoke that the Count was looking tense.

Equally there was almost a beseeching look on his face which was more than understandable.

Very slowly and speaking extremely good English, although with a slight accent, the Count told Linetta of the present situation in Samosia.

He did not exaggerate, but it was obvious that every word he spoke was the truth.

It would be impossible for anyone to question it.

He spoke for nearly ten minutes and then, as if the full horror of his country's situation had exhausted him, he sat down again in his chair having stood up while he was speaking.

There was a silence and then Linetta said in a small voice,

"Are you really asking me to marry a man I have never seen and, in fact, never heard of until this moment?"

"There is no other way," the Count answered, "to save Samosia. I assure you that a great number of people will die and those who remain under the Russian yoke will be desperately unhappy and persecuted for the rest of their lives."

Linetta drew in her breath.

Then she turned to her father.

He did not speak, but put out his hand towards her.

She rose from her chair to sit down on the floor at his feet.

Then, as if she was ignoring the other two men in the room, she looked up at him and murmured,

"Tell me, Papa, what do you want me to do?"

"Of course I would want you to stay here with us," he answered. "At the same time have we the strength in our hearts to let those people suffer and perhaps die simply because they are not strong enough to withstand the greed and arrogance of the Russians?"

He paused for a moment before he added,

"I know only too well that they are fully determined eventually to take over all of the Balkans and Samosia is vital to them as it is so close to the Mediterranean Sea."

Again there was a poignant silence.

Then Linetta asked,

"But Papa, is there no other country the Russians are afraid of, except for Great Britain?"

"Unfortunately," he replied, "there is no one who has the power that we have and I have always believed that eventually the Czar will attempt to seize India."

There was a murmur from the Count as he said that, which told those listening that Prince Vladimir was right.

There was no doubt that India was the prize that the Russians desired before anything else.

"So is there no one else," Linetta asked, "who could marry Prince Ivor and perhaps enjoy the status and power it would bring her?"

She was looking at the Count as she was speaking, but it was the Earl who answered her.

"I went to Windsor Castle yesterday," he said, "and found, as I expected, that Her Majesty had been worried that this subject would soon arise."

There was silence for a moment.

"She had gone very carefully through her relations to find one who she could send," he continued, "as she has sent quite a number of others to Europe to save them from the avarice and greed of the Russians."

He paused before he went on,

"But Her Majesty professed that she had searched most diligently amongst her family and could find no one available until unexpectedly she remembered your father."

"I thought no one would remember the commotion that I caused over twenty years ago," Prince Vladimir said with a sarcastic note in his voice.

"It would be difficult for anyone who knew you well to forget you," the Earl pointed out. "Although you may think I am exaggerating, I have often thought of you and had wished that you were still in London so that we could laugh together as we did in the good old days when anything unusual occurred."

"And now something unusual *has* occurred," Prince Vladimir said abruptly. "And frankly I am not amused."

His daughter looked up at him.

Then she rose to her feet and walked to the open French window.

She stood gazing out at the garden and the fountain, not only at the beauty but the peace of the scene in front of her.

She could not help thinking that a number of people just like herself might be looking in the same way at their gardens and their land, knowing that, if the Russians took it over, their lives would never be the same again.

Perhaps they would be happier if they died than if they continued to live, losing all their dearest friends and most prized possessions.

Then Linetta looked up at the sky.

Instinctively she was praying to God to whom she had said her prayers since she was a small child.

'Help me! Please help me!' she prayed. 'Help me, God, to take the right decision and not one that will make other people suffer unnecessarily.'

Even as she said the words, she knew the answer in her heart.

Somehow, because she believed it came from God Himself, she turned slowly and came back into the middle of the room.

The three men had not moved since she had risen.

But their eyes were on her as she walked towards her father.

She put her hand on her father's shoulder and he covered it with his.

Then she said very quietly,

"Ever since I was a very small girl, Papa, you have taught me to think of other people rather than myself and I feel that it would be wrong and perhaps wicked to let a lot of people die and be tortured because I will not do my best – to help them."

"I thought you would say that, my darling one," he sighed.

There was a note of pain in his voice.

"I want, Papa," Linetta went on, "to make certain conditions. I don't feel that I am asking too much, so I beg of you to listen to me without prejudice."

"Of course," the Earl agreed. "We will listen to anything you have to say. We will try in every possible way to make your task, if you undertake it, an easy one."

There was an expectant hush in the room before Linetta began in a very low voice,

"I have always believed that one day I would find a man who would love me for myself as I would love him. And if we married, I would be as happy as my father and mother have been."

She hesitated for a moment before she went on,

"When I was old enough to understand it, Papa told me how horrified not only his family but the Society they moved in were – when he fell in love with – my mother."

There was a break in her voice as she added,

"Because they loved each other – so much, they ran away from all that was familiar to them – and everything they had been brought up to believe was their world where they each played such – a vital part."

She drew in her breath and her fingers tightened on her father's as she said,

"I never imagined that two people could be – so very happy or that my home was so filled with love that it has seemed to me impossible to ever want to leave it or to try and find someone I would love in the same way – as my mother loves my father."

Both the Earl and the Count were deeply moved by the way she spoke, but said nothing.

After a moment Linetta took out her handkerchief and wiped away a tear and then she went on,

"You will therefore understand, at least I hope you will, that I cannot marry a man I have never seen, someone I might dislike – or even hate rather than love."

"I can understand that," the Count said very quietly before anyone else could speak.

"I thought perhaps you would," Linetta murmured. "So I am asking for a little time before I make my final decision."

"Time is the one thing that is difficult to give you," the Count answered. "As his Lordship well knows, the Russians are very swift in their movements. In fact they had begun their work in Samosia and achieved quite a lot of progress before we realised just how dangerous they can be."

"I have read in the newspapers all about the way the Russians are behaving," Linetta said. "It horrified me – even though I had no idea it might have anything personal – to do with me. At the same time I have my own life and future to consider."

She glanced at her father before she added,

"Therefore I cannot say 'yes' to your proposition of marrying the Prince until I have seen him and know if it is possible for me ever to be his close friend let alone his wife."

The Count made a helpless gesture with his hands.

"Then what can we do?" he asked.

"That is what I am going to tell you."

Linetta looked at her father again as if he gave her strength.

He knew from the way her fingers trembled in his that she was very nervous.

"Take things slowly, my darling," he said. "We are all listening and you have every right, if you are to make such a great sacrifice, to ask for anything you want at this moment."

Linetta turned to the Count.

"Tell me," she asked him, "although perhaps it is a question I should have asked before, have you a family of your own?"

"I have indeed," the Count replied. "My wife and I are happily married and we have three children. My eldest daughter is fourteen, her sister is twelve and I have a son who will be ten years old on his next birthday."

There was a distinct note of pride in his voice that was rather touching.

Linetta actually smiled before she said,

"Then that would surely make things easier because I want to ask if you will take me to Samosia and let me stay with you before anyone finds out who I am. I could come as a Governess, who will teach your children music."

The Count stared at her in astonishment and so did the Earl.

"As a Governess!" the Count exclaimed, almost as if he thought that he could not have understood what she had said to him.

"I learnt music from my mother and, as my father knows, I am a very good at the piano. I will stay with you and your children will learn from me while you arrange for me to see Prince Ivor and perhaps even speak to him."

The three men stared at her.

After a moment she declared,

"I will then, as quickly as possible, say 'yes' or 'no' to your proposition."

"Is that possible?" the Count asked incredulously.

It was then that Prince Vladimir spoke.

"I think it is an extremely sensible and reasonable suggestion," he said. "If my daughter feels that life would be intolerable with the Prince, then she has every right to refuse him and she can return to England in safety."

"I have a better idea than that," Linetta said. "In fact the idea of it is coming to me in a way that I feel is in answer to my prayers – rather than what I have thought out on my own."

She looked again at her father as if asking him to believe in her.

He smiled at her as he asked,

"Tell me exactly what you want, my darling. It is you who must make the final decision one way or another. I know that the Count will make things as easy as possible for you in Samosia. But then, as always happens in Royal circles to a certain extent, his hands are tied."

"I am aware of that," Linetta replied. "Therefore what I want is for me to go ahead with Count Unkar and have perhaps a week or so with his children and see the Prince as much as he can arrange for me to do so."

Her father nodded and she went on,

"By the time the week is over I would like, if at all possible, for you, Papa, as His Royal Highness, to be at the Port with an English ship which, if I stay, will carry my wedding gown, but if not then it will take you and me back home."

The three men stared at her in surprise.

Then Linetta carried on,

"What it amounts to is that either you, Papa, come ashore bearing your own name as Your Royal Highness the Prince of Leiningen or else I leave without any difficulties and return to England with my father, the Baron."

As if he could not help it, Prince Vladimir gave a laugh.

"Brilliant!" he exclaimed. "Only you, darling, could have thought of anything quite so clever, something which, if properly arranged and planned could happen without any trouble or interference."

He paused for a moment before he added,

"Of course I would wish to give you away at your Wedding. I want to impress the Russians and the people

48

you will rule over and I must therefore take up the position again that I threw away when I married your mother."

"If the Union Jack is flying at your Wedding," the Count interposed, "I promise you by the next morning the Russians will be moving out of Samosia and back into the Principalities they have already conquered."

"Do you then accept my proposition?" she asked, looking at him.

"I think there is only one place worthy of you, Lady Linetta," the Count said, "and that is on a throne!"

"I agree with that," the Earl joined in. "In fact I am astonished that you should be thinking so clearly and so positively at what we can only describe as a few minutes' notice."

He smiled as he turned to Prince Vladimir and said,

"She is so incredibly like you, Vladimir. When she was speaking, I kept thinking that I was listening to you at Oxford and how you astonished the class by expressing what the Professor was trying to teach us and making it so much clearer than the old boy could manage himself!"

Prince Vladimir laughed.

"That all happened a long time ago. But I am glad you think that my daughter takes after me and needless to say I am very proud of her."

"So you think that I have made the right decision – Papa?" Linetta asked in a low voice.

"You have made a decision that no one could say was unjust or unfair. Indeed I could not have thought of anything better myself."

Linetta smiled.

"That is high praise indeed, Papa. But you must promise me that you will come to my Wedding because, however charming the Prince might be, I would not marry anyone unless you were there to give me away."

"I will not only come myself to your Wedding," the Prince answered, "but I will bring your mother because I don't want to be without her and it is only right that she should take her place as the Princess of Leiningen, which she has always been but never claimed."

"But, of course, you must bring Mama with you!" Linetta exclaimed. "If anything would induce me to marry the Prince even if he is not as handsome as I want him to be, it would be because you, Papa, and Mama have hidden yourselves away for too long. If you came back to the world in Samosia, then I think it would be good for both of you."

Prince Vladimir laughed again.

"You see," he said, turning to the Earl, "out of the mouths of babes and sucklings one always gets the truth."

There was silence for a moment.

"Although I am quite happy as I am," he continued, "perhaps there is work for me to do somewhere in the world, which would be of advantage to more people than I can employ on the small piece of land that belongs to me here."

"I think that you and your daughter are both exactly what Samosia wants at this moment," the Count said. "I can only thank you, Lady Linetta, for the brilliant way in which you have solved this problem and your bravery in saying that you will come to Samosia."

Now he took Linetta's hand in his and kissed it in the French fashion.

She smiled at him before she said,

"You must not forget that if I don't like the Prince and there is always the chance he may dislike me, I must leave without any difficulty – and without any fuss."

"I promise everything shall be exactly as you have asked for it," the Count said. "Of course, if I do my part of the bargain, I am very sure that the Earl, in his important position as a British Secretary of State, will do his."

"I don't think that there will be any difficulties in my carrying out exactly all that Lady Linetta has asked of us," the Earl replied. "Now, as we have been nervous that we might have left here empty-handed, I would now like to drink a toast to the future Princess, or maybe even 'Queen' would be a better word, of Samosia."

Prince Vladimir released his daughter's hand and rose to go to the side table and pour out the champagne.

Linetta walked to the window again and looked up into the sky.

She was thanking God in her heart for what she thought had been the answer to her fervent prayers.

Because there had been no opposition and they had accepted everything she had asked for, she felt as if God or perhaps one of His archangels was hovering over her and guiding her.

At the same time she could not help feeling in the depths of her heart that there was a question at present still unanswered.

It was –

'What was the Prince like and would she find the love she was seeking?'

Her father then poured out the champagne and the Count and the Earl walked to the side table to pick up their glasses.

As they turned around to raise them to Linetta, it was to find that she had vanished.

There was only the sunshine pouring in through the open window.

"Your daughter is brilliant," the Earl enthused. "I confess now that I was very nervous when we came here. I thought that like many young girls she would be hysterical at the idea of leaving home and marrying someone she had not even seen."

"I feel certain that she will like Prince Ivor," the Count said, as if reassuring himself. "I have always found him a charming young man. He is very cosmopolitan in many ways."

He smiled before he continued,

"In fact he was educated in France for some years and finally went for a year to a University in Germany."

Both men listening thought that this ensured that he would not be too insular or ignorant of the world outside his own country.

Prince Vladimir then toasted his two visitors and the future of Samosia.

Then he left them alone.

He went from the study along the corridor to the drawing room where he knew he would find his wife.

He was not surprised that Linetta was with her.

As he walked in through the door, Princess Crystal, as she should have been called, rose to her feet.

"Linetta has been telling me what has happened, Vladimir," his wife said. "Oh, darling, must we lose her?"

"I don't believe," he replied, "that we are losing a daughter, but gaining a son-in-law and exploring a country I have never visited which I believe we will find extremely interesting."

As he was speaking, he put his arm round his wife and pulled her close to him.

"You are not to be upset," he urged. "This is Fate and I cannot help thinking that perhaps it will make us take our rightful place in the world again because we could give many people the happiness we have passed on here to just a small number of those who know us."

Crystal looked up at him with concern in her eyes.

He thought as she did so that she was even lovelier than when he had first married her.

She had always been a beauty but somehow instead of losing that elusive beauty which had shone behind the footlights and as she had become older it had softened and grown in his eyes even more spectacularly than it had been before.

Linetta was very like her.

And she had inherited her father's strong as well as elegant body.

In his opinion she was superb on a horse.

"I know whatever had been arranged, if it has your approval, darling," Crystal was now saying, "it will be the right thing to do and as we are English we must help those who are menaced by the cruel and wicked Russians."

"That is just what Queen Victoria would say," her husband replied. "Therefore, my darling, there is no need for you and I to be upset because our beloved Linetta is leaving for another part of the world."

"Now it is so easy to move about either by sea or in a train," Crystal said, "we can visit Linetta whenever she needs us just as, if it all goes wrong, she could come home rapidly to us."

Prince Vladimir kissed his wife's cheek.

"You always say the right thing, my darling," he told her. "Linetta has said the same to our two guests. In fact I am not exaggerating when I say that the Count, who is the Secretary of State for Foreign Affairs for Samosia is captivated by her."

Linetta, who had been listening, laughed,

"I am so glad that someone is and, of course, what they hope is that the Prince of Samosia will be enchanted by me and me by him."

"Naturally that is what we all want," her father answered. "But I am astonished, my precious, that you should have been so clever and thought out what you could accept so quickly."

"I only hope that I will be able to play the piano and teach the Count's children as well as Mama has taught me," Linetta said.

"You play beautifully and you will certainly have a far bigger audience to applaud you than you have here."

Before Linetta could answer her father, her mother said in a low and rather frightened voice,

"You are quite certain that she will be safe in the Balkans? I have read about the fighting that there has been there and the way the Russians have conquered so many Principalities by the most unfair and unpleasant means."

"She will be absolutely safe just as long as she is entitled to fly the Union Jack," he replied. "You are not to be frightened, my darling. I promise you if there is one country the Russians fear it is Great Britain. In fact they just cannot afford to fight us more than they have done already."

He paused for a moment before he went on,

"I should not be surprised if, after Linetta marries the Prince of Samosia, they are asked to St. Petersburg to meet the Czar!"

Linetta gave a little cry.

"That is one thing I would adore. At the same time he might easily poison me if I have prevented him from conquering Samosia!"

Her father smiled.

"You can be certain that he would not do anything that would make Queen Victoria angrier with the Russians than she is already."

"I will have a gown made entirely of Union Jacks," Linetta laughed.

Her mother gave a little cry.

"One thing we have to think of quickly," she said, "is Linetta's trousseau. Everyone knows that, if she is to leave at once for Samosia, she will most certainly need a great number of new dresses both for the daytime and the evening."

She paused before she questioned her husband,

"And how are we to going to buy them sitting here without a shop capable of providing an ordinary trousseau let alone a Royal one?"

"I can tell you what we will do," he said hurriedly. "If we have a week in which to follow Linetta, we will start off as quickly as possible in a yacht that I know I will be able to borrow from a friend of mine who lives just outside Plymouth."

"I know who you mean," his wife replied. "I am sure that he will be only too pleased to let us have his yacht just as long as we don't run it aground or sink it by some means!"

"I hope that we will do neither, but we can stop in France on our way to the Mediterranean."

There was silence for a moment.

"I am sure at Marseilles," Prince Vladimir went on, "we will find a great number of gowns which will enhance our daughter's beauty and, of course, make her look the part she is to play as the Prince of Samosia's wife."

"You are going much too fast, Papa," Linetta said quickly.

She smiled as she added,

"I have to be quite certain that I want to marry the Prince. If you buy me an expensive trousseau and I decide

55

against it, I will only have the horses, the pigs and the dogs to admire it when I wear it at home!"

"I am sure that they would be most impressed!" her father answered laughingly. "At the same time, my darling, I am banking on the fact that you will sit on the throne of Samosia."

He smiled at her as he continued,

"Your mother and I will find it entrancing to watch you gaining the hearts of your people and making them the envy of all the other Principalities in the Balkans."

Linetta laughed.

"You are asking too much, Papa, but I will do my best as you well know. As your daughter I have a very good start when the race begins."

"Your mother and I are so very proud of you," he told her. "Now we really must go back and entertain our guests before they start their journey back to London."

His wife nodded.

Then Prince Vladimir said,

"I think that the Count has arranged for the ship in which he came to England to sail as quickly as possible to Plymouth."

His wife stared at him.

"Are you now suggesting that they are to stay the night?" she asked.

"I don't think the ship will be here until very late," he replied. "They will therefore have to stay with us and leave tomorrow."

"Do you mean that they will be taking Linetta with them?" Crystal demanded.

"I am afraid so," he replied quietly.

For a moment it seemed as if his wife was about to protest.

Then, as she met his eyes, she realised that he was thinking it would be a mistake for Linetta to have time to think too much about her position and perhaps change her mind.

Having made the decision it was so vital that they should carry the plan out immediately.

Otherwise, in a very human fashion, doubts would step in and other options would seem better.

And then the whole business would have to start all over again.

Because she knew exactly what he was thinking, Crystal said,

"All right, darling! It will be a bit of a rush, but I daresay we will manage. As you say when we join Linetta we can take her some of the beautiful dresses that France makes automatically and which no one else can equal."

Again Prince Vladimir kissed his wife's cheek.

He knew because they were so close and because their thoughts were always readable by the other, that she was doing what he wished without any argument simply because she loved him and wanted to go along with his and Linetta's decision.

And not to think of herself at all or in this case of her daughter.

'If only Linetta will be as lucky as I have been,' he thought to himself.

Taking his wife by the hand, Prince Vladimir drew her back into the drawing room to where the guests were waiting for them.

*

It was late that night and long after their guests and Linetta had gone to bed that Crystal slipped into the large four-poster bed where her husband was waiting for her.

"I have now turned out every single cupboard in the house," she said, "to find dresses that would be suitable for a Governess."

She paused before she carried on,

"Because Linetta is so beautiful and I have always dressed her to please you rather than spend time choosing the long-lasting clothes that most girls wear in the country and she will, I believe, Governess or no Governess, look very lovely."

"You are so marvellous, my darling," he said. "No one else could be as clever as you have been. I have an idea that any other mother would be screaming hysterically by now or protesting violently against the speed, which is unfortunately very necessary."

Crystal laughed.

"We want our darling daughter to do us credit," she replied. "As she is representing Great Britain as well, what she wears is very important."

"Has there ever been a woman who has not thought that clothes matter more than anything else?" he asked.

His wife moved closer to him and his arms went round her.

"Every time you come this close to me," he said, "I think I love you more than I loved you five minutes ago and certainly a year ago and the year before that."

"I know what you are saying," his wife answered. "You know that I love you so much. You fill my whole world and there is no one else but you."

She gave a little sigh before she added,

"At the same time, darling, we do want Linetta to be happy too. But how can she be happy with a man she has never seen before?"

"I am just praying that like us she will see him and fall in love as I fell in love with you the very moment you appeared on the stage and played the music that seemed to capture my heart completely."

"I love you when you say things like that," his wife answered. "It all happened a long time ago and now, my precious husband, we have to think of our children and pray that they will be as happy as we have been."

She looked up at him as she asked,

"Did you ever regret giving up your prime position in London Society and being feted by those distinguished people?"

It was a question he had heard many times before.

And Prince Vladimir replied,

"I just don't believe that there is another man in the whole world who has been as happy as I have been. All I can ask God is that Linetta finds the real love as we found it the moment we met."

His arm round her tightened as he went on,

"I knew then that I could not live without you and the years that we have been here seem to have flown past simply because we have been so happy."

"It has been like Heaven to be with you," Crystal answered. "There have just been a few times when I have thought that perhaps my talent at playing so successfully as I did in London has been wasted."

She paused before she said,

"But now I know it is that same music which will perhaps enter the heart of the Prince of Samosia and make him fall in love with Linetta in the same way as you fell in love with me."

"It was not only your music," he breathed. "It was your lovely face, your perfect eyes and your soft lips."

He kissed her as was speaking.

Then, as they clung closely together, there was no need for words.

CHAPTER FOUR

They left very early in the morning and found the Samosian ship waiting for them at the Port of Plymouth.

When they went aboard, Prince Vladimir looked to see whether the cabin that his daughter was to occupy was comfortable.

He found it excellent in every possible way.

He shook hands with the ship's Officers and the crew.

When they reached the Saloon, Linetta clung to her father and said,

"I do wish you were coming with me, Papa, but you promise, on your word of honour, that you will not be very far behind."

"I was thinking it over in the night," he said, "and I have decided that we will be at the Port that is nearest to Samosia in a shorter time than you would be expecting. We can easily wait on board, but you may not be able to meet us."

He smiled affectionately at his daughter before he went on,

"But remember that within three days at the most we will be waiting for you if you join us or if you come and tell me that I am to come ashore with you and present you to the country as the relative of Her Majesty."

Linetta hid her face against her father's shoulder.

"I hate leaving you, Papa," she whispered. "But I feel I had to do the right thing."

"You have done exactly the right thing," her father replied, "and what I would expect of someone with Royal Blood in her veins. And remember that I love you very much and always will. I am so very proud of my beautiful girl."

There were tears welling up in Linetta's eyes when she said her goodbyes to her father before he finally went ashore.

But she stood on deck waving to him as the ship moved away from Plymouth.

She knew that he would not only keep his word in coming to Samosia as soon as possible but he would also be praying that they would save Samosia and the Russians would be forced, once they knew that the country had the Queen's blessing, to retreat.

Linetta waved to her father until they were well out into the open sea and she could see him no more.

Then she went to the Saloon where she knew that the Count would be waiting for her.

She had also been informed by a Steward that their breakfast was ready.

They had been in such a hurry to leave that she had barely had time to kiss her mother tenderly.

Then she had to hurry herself to the carriage that was waiting for her, drawn by four of her father's finest horses.

Her mother had refused to go to Plymouth and see her leave.

"It is always upsetting," she said, "to say goodbye to people, especially those you love. Therefore I am letting you do it one at a time rather than Papa and I together to kiss you goodbye."

Linetta knew exactly what her mother meant.

She merely held her very closely and said,

"You promise you will come with Papa to Samosia. If things go wrong I will feel so much happier if you are there to support me."

"I will be praying that everything will go right," her mother replied. "As you know, my darling one, you can always rely on me. And I will be bringing with me all the prettiest and most attractive clothes that you could possibly desire for your trousseau."

It was impossible for Linetta to answer because she was close to tears.

But she forced herself not to cry.

She walked resolutely to the carriage where her father was waiting for her.

He was driving himself and did not speak to her until he knew that she had composed herself and was no longer feeling tearful.

Now that the ship was finally out of sight, he turned away and walked slowly back to where his carriage was waiting.

He was asking himself, as he had asked a thousand times throughout the night, whether he was doing the right thing in allowing his daughter to go to Samosia alone.

But he was confident that the Count would look after her and she would be with his family, which he was certain were as charming as he was himself.

When breakfast was over and Linetta had managed to talk quite sensibly to the Count about what lay ahead, she said,

"Now we have to get down to work. Although I am afraid it will be boring for you, we have very little time to do all I want."

The Count looked at her with surprise.

"I don't know what you mean, Lady Linetta," he asked. "What work do we have to do?"

Linetta laughed.

"You don't suppose," she answered, "that I intend to walk ashore at Samosia and not be able to talk to the Prince or any of his people in their own language?"

The Count stared at her and then admitted,

"Of course it is extremely remiss of me not to have realised that. I will teach you all I can in the short space of time we have to do so."

"I don't think that it will be as difficult as all that," Linetta replied. "Papa sent me to Berlin for six months so I speak perfect German."

She paused a moment before continuing,

"I also spent a few months in Italy and much longer in Greece because I was so entranced with all the Gods and Goddesses after I had read dozens of books about them before I actually arrived."

The Count stared at her again.

Then he enquired,

"Are you telling me that you can speak Greek as well?"

"Yes, I speak Greek quite fluently," Linetta replied, "although I don't like the language as I find it rather too emotional."

"Then there is really no need for me to teach you anything," the Count said. "As I expect you know already, Lady Linetta, the Balkan languages are a mixture of all the countries that border them, but most especially Greece and Austria."

"I expect they have little twiddly-bits of their own," Linetta laughed. "I think from this moment that we must speak your language and nothing else."

"I do admire you as one of the most sensible young women I have ever met in my whole life," the Count said in his own language. "I can only hope that I am as good a conversationalist as you are a pianist!"

"Thank you for the compliment, Count, and let me add I cannot have too many!"

They were both laughing as they started her first session.

Fortunately the Count had some interesting books with him that Linetta said she would like to read quietly on her own.

She promised that she would make a list of all the words that she did not understand.

When they retired to bed that evening, the Count, having conversed fluently at dinner, thought that he had been most fortunate in having the company of anyone so clever, as well as so lovely as Linetta.

He could not help feeling that Prince Ivor would be blind, deaf and dumb if he did not fall in love with her the moment he met her.

But there had, of course, been some very attractive visitors to The Palace of Samosia in the past.

Although it was not in his nature to pry or to ask awkward questions, the Count could not help being aware that there had been several charming and attractive women the Prince had rather obviously been somewhat infatuated with.

But none of them had lasted very long.

Although there had always been new faces to take their place, the Prince had been extremely careful never to cause a scenario that the Russians could make a scandal over.

*

Before they reached the end of the Mediterranean and they were travelling very fast, the Count thought that Linetta was not only the prettiest girl he had ever seen in his life but also the most intelligent.

She insisted on talking only in his language.

After the first day on board she was making very few mistakes and by the end of the second day hardly any at all.

'I would not believe it if I had read it in a book,' the Count thought to himself as he went to bed.

He was now aware, if he had not known it before, that Linetta had her father's brain as well as her mother's beauty and musical talent.

When they arrived in the Aegean Sea, it was with the greatest difficulty Linetta did not beg the Count to let her stop for a short while to explore the Greek islands, particularly those that were connected with the Gods and Goddesses she had always admired so much.

"It is agonising," she said to the Count, "to pass the Island where Apollo was born which I am told still has a number of fine statues to see that came from the Temple erected to him."

"I am sure that the Prince will want to show you Apollo's Island himself," the Count suggested.

Linetta gave him a sharp glance.

"Are you now telling me that the Prince is really interested in Greek mythology?" she asked. "Or are you, because I am so infatuated with Greece, bringing him in just to please me?"

"I have been very careful," the Count answered, "to tell you only the truth. Like your father you have such a sharp mind that I feel no one could lie to you without you knowing it. It was something I felt about him when we were talking together."

"You are quite right, Count. Papa always tells the truth and, if it is not the truth, he says so."

She could remember when she was quite a small child her father saying,

'If there is one thing I dislike it is lies. Tell me the truth however much you think it may upset me or make me angry, but never, never lie to me because it is something I despise and hate more than anything else.'

"I will always tell the truth," Linetta said simply, "because I was brought up to do so. But I am afraid some other people are not so well-educated as I have been."

The Count could not help thinking that this was due to the fact that Prince Vladimir, who was an exceedingly clever man, had few other attractions in the retreat where he and his wife had hidden themselves away for so many years.

So it was not surprising that their children must have been very advanced for their age.

'How could I have been so fortunate,' the Count asked himself again, 'to find someone so beautiful and so intelligent for Samosia?'

He smiled to himself and almost said aloud,

'If the Prince is not bowled over by her, then I will resign from my post and leave someone cleverer than I am to find him a different sort of wife.'

He was, however, certain in his own mind that the Prince would find Linetta irresistible.

The only real problem was whether she would feel the same about him.

As they travelled at a great speed past the Greek Islands and had their first glimpse of the Balkans, Linetta was silent.

The Count realised that now the moment was near when she would meet the man she must marry or leave him and his country in the hands of the Russians.

It was a very very hard decision for a young girl to make.

He only wished that he could do something to help her more than he had done already.

'At least,' he thought, 'she can now speak the same language as the Prince. She can converse with any of his people from the lowest to the highest.'

But was that enough?

The question seemed to repeat itself over and over again in his mind.

*

At the ship docked at the Port and he saw a number of people waiting to meet him, he felt that the real drama in which he had so completely entangled himself was about to begin.

Linetta was as conscious as he was that 'the curtain was going up'.

And as the principle performer in the play she must not make a mistake.

She dressed herself carefully in the simplest clothes she possessed.

She wore a plain undecorated hat over her shining golden hair.

Although she had to go ashore with the Count as there was no one else with them, she knew that she must keep in the background as she had come to Samosia only as a Governess to his children.

He realised that she was behaving as he might have expected of her.

In fact she was playing her part brilliantly and he was determined to do the same.

Having warmly greeted his friends and colleagues who were waiting on the quay for him, he now realised that Linetta was standing a little way back behind him by the luggage.

Those who had come to meet him were looking at her somewhat curiously.

"I must tell you," he said, "that I have brought back with me an English Governess for my family. I thought it was time for all of us to speak the language of Her Majesty the Queen of Great Britain who, I hope and pray, will help us in the way we want her to do."

The Comptroller of the Port from his office window looked at him sharply and then whispered into the Count's ear,

"Has the Queen agreed?"

"I will tell you later," the Count said. "All I want at the moment is to go home to see if my wife and family are safe and well."

"That is what we all want," one of the men who had come to meet him added. "The Russians are, in fact, a great deal nearer than they were when you left."

"Tell me all about it as soon as we get back to the house," the Count said. "As you know I will want to hear every detail of what has been happening while I have been away."

As he spoke, he walked to a carriage and beckoned to Linetta to join him.

They had just seated themselves on the back seat when two of his junior officials jumped in the carriage to sit themselves opposite them.

The Count knew that the rest of them would bring his luggage and Linetta's with them.

He sat back comfortably on the upholstered seat of the carriage and demanded,

"Now tell me the worst."

"I am afraid it *is* the worst," the man beside him replied.

"Why? What has happened," the Count enquired.

"Because a Russian Regiment is now several miles nearer than when you left," the man told him. "And their infiltration has increased enormously."

"Has His Royal Highness done anything about it?" the Count enquired.

"What can he do?" the man answered. "We have of course enormously strengthened the number of our soldiers on duty especially at night. But I am afraid the infiltration of Russians in one disguise or another is increasing day by day."

There was silence.

Then the other man who had not spoken previously spoke up,

"I am only hoping that you have brought us back good news, Count. It is what we are all praying for and longing to hear."

"I think it is only correct," the Count replied, "for me to speak to His Royal Highness first."

The two men laughed.

"We had a small bet that was what you would say. Although we came to meet you, we knew that we would not learn any more than if we had stayed at home."

The Count laughed too.

"Well, that's the way it goes," he replied. "As you know, I try to keep my feet firmly on the ground and not raise people's hopes unnecessarily."

The two men gave a sharp glance to each other at his reply.

At the same time they felt, as Linetta was present, that they could not press him as they would have done if they had been alone with him.

Instead they told him more of what was happening in the City and that the Prince had bought several more horses that were the admiration of everyone who came to see them.

"I would be a great deal happier," one man said, "if the money had been spent on larger guns. But, if you ask me, His Royal Highness is expecting you to bring back good news. He could not bear to lose these horses that went up for sale when their owner died."

"We will soon have to be building new stables, I can see that," the Count joked.

The two men agreed with him.

The drive did not take long as the City of Samosia was only ten miles from the sea.

Gazing out of the window, Linetta thought that the olive trees and the wide expanse of fertile open land were very beautiful.

When she then had her first sight of the City in the distance, she was impressed by the great number of towers there were, besides the spires that she knew must belong to Churches.

The Count informed her that the City was no less than the Capital of Samosia.

When they drove nearer still, she had her first sight of a huge Cathedral and she felt that The Palace itself could not be too far away.

It was on the outskirts of the City and had been apparently built on top of ground that rose at the far end of open land where there were no other buildings.

Then their carriage turned round a sharp corner and there, dominating the skyline, she saw a magnificent and very beautiful Palace.

There was no need for Linetta to ask the Count if she was right that it was where His Royal Highness Prince Ivor lived.

She then had her first glimpse of the flags flying on the roof and numerous sentries in colourful uniforms at the gates.

These they passed and then a little further on they came to a gate where there were no sentries.

They led, she could see, to a grand house that was also raised from the ground to almost the same height as The Palace.

To her surprise, as the gate opened up, the horses pulling their carriage passed in and walked up the winding drive to what she realised was a large and fine-looking house.

"We left our carriages in your drive," one of the men said to the Count. "But we will not worry you now to tell us what we are longing to hear because we know that you will be wanting to talk to your wife. Will it worry you if we come back in say an hour or two?"

"It depends if I have seen His Royal Highness in that time or not," the Count replied. "As I have said I must tell him first what has happened. I only hope that he will be at The Palace this evening."

The two men looked at each other.

"I think," one of them said, "His Royal Highness was going South to see various people who he thinks might help us with the Russian menace. It is getting worse day by day and he thought that he had friends who might assist him in some way or another."

"Then I hope he will not be away long," the Count replied. "I promise you the moment I have spoken to him, I will be free to talk to you."

"I suppose that we have to be thankful for small mercies," one man said. "But, as you can imagine, we are all extremely curious and that includes our wives and our sweethearts for that matter."

They all laughed at this.

The two men did not then enter the house when the carriage stopped outside it, but walked off to the stables that were close by.

The Count led the way into what Linetta thought was a very impressive and charming house.

She could not help commenting as they pulled up in front of it,

"Surely, Count, you are most fortunate to have a house as grand as this next to The Palace itself."

"I was offered it when it became empty after His Royal Highness's mother died," the Count told her. "The people thought, perhaps in an over-exaggerated way, that, as I was the Secretary of State for Foreign Affairs, I might somehow be more of a protection to the Prince if I was living close to him than if I was at the other end of the City."

Linetta thought, although she did not say so, that it must be terrifying to have the Russians so near, menacing not only the City itself but the Ruler of the country.

There was no time for her to respond to anything that the Count was saying before there was a loud cry of delight.

A very attractive woman followed by three children came running rapidly from one of the rooms towards the Count.

"You are back! You are back!" the woman cried, as she flung her arms round him. "I have been so worried while you have been away and it is so wonderful that you are here again."

"It is exactly where I always want to be and that is the truth," the Count said as he kissed his wife.

Then he kissed his three enchanting children.

The little girls were both very pretty with long hair hanging almost to their waists.

The boy looked very strong and athletic.

Linetta was sure that he would end up being as tall as his father.

She had been impressed by the fact that the Count was nearly as tall as her father who dwarfed quite a number of men who called on them.

She thought it might be amusing if she did marry the Prince to live in a City or a town and not have to be isolated, as she had been ever since she had been born in Devon.

Now that she understood why her father was there and why he had not wished for anyone to know his real name, she could understand that he had been very clever in finding a place where no one would be particularly curious about him and where those who were curious were unable to find him.

The Count introduced Linetta to his wife and three children.

He told them that she had been so anxious to visit Samosia and he had asked her to stay with them and to teach the children piano at which she was undoubtedly one of the best players he had ever heard.

Linetta saw the Countess look rather sceptical as if she thought that, because she was so young, this must be an exaggeration.

At the same time the children were delighted.

"I love music," the elder girl enthused. "Although I have had lessons, I always thought that our teachers were not particularly brilliant and I have asked Papa if, when I am a little older, I could go to school in Paris."

She smiled before she went on,

"I believe that there are a great number of brilliant performers who, in their spare time, teach pupils from the Universities and schools."

"When you have listened to Miss Lane," the Count said, "you will know that there is no need for you to go to France!"

It was not the first time that Linetta had heard him use the name they had called her aboard ship.

But somehow when the Countess and the children called her 'Miss Lane' it made her want to laugh.

It was her father who had suggested that it was the nearest to her real name he could think of.

And it was one she would find easy to remember.

That was indeed true.

Equally Linetta found herself almost starting a little at her new name and finding it difficult to reply instantly when someone addressed her as 'Miss Lane'.

She was then shown into her bedroom which she was aware was quite a bit larger than was usually occupied by a Governess.

It overlooked the garden and the fields that sloped down to the wide open land they had driven through from the sea.

When later she went out into the garden because the children wanted to show her a small artificial lake where they were able to bathe, it was then that she had a better glimpse of The Palace.

74

She thought, as she had when she had first seen it from the carriage, that it was magnificent.

She wondered if she would see the Prince, but there was no sign of anyone in The Palace garden.

Linetta learnt later at dinner that the Prince was not at home but visiting friends, as the Count had been told, because he was eliciting their help.

"If you are to ask me," the Countess said, "we want someone of greater status to help us than those His Royal Highness is visiting."

There was silence for the moment.

"Every day I am told stories by the staff," she went on, "of how the Russians are making trouble in the City and creating quite an uproar amongst some of the men who should know better than to side with our enemies however badly they think they might have been treated by us."

She spoke sharply and the Count replied,

"I would hope when I talk to His Royal Highness that things will be better than they are at the moment."

"They are getting worse and worse," his wife said, "and quite frankly, darling, I am really afraid."

She drew in her breath before she added,

"I think that it would be wise for you to take us to somewhere safe. You know that our friends in Vienna are always asking us to visit them."

"We may be able to do that a little later on," the Count said.

"If we wait too long, it may be impossible for us to leave. In fact we could all be in prison," the Countess replied.

The Count put his fingers to his lips as if to warn her not to say too much in front of the servants.

But the Countess carried on regardless,

"I am just incredibly frightened! Frightened for the children's sake as well as our own. I have been praying as everyone else has in the City that you would bring us some good news from Her Majesty Queen Victoria."

"I have to say to you exactly the same as I have told everyone else," the Count said, "that I must speak to the Prince before I can tell you what happened while I was in England."

He sighed before he continued,

"At the same time, my dearest, I don't want you to be depressed or intimidated."

"So how could we be anything else?" the Countess asked. "The Russians are reinforcing their Regiments only a few miles from here. I am told that the trouble they are causing in the City itself is appalling."

"I know! I *do* know!" he replied. "I have heard it already. But I think that is the job of the Prime Minister and the Cabinet and not mine!"

"It is your job to protect us and the children," his wife asserted.

"If you go on talking like this you will scare them," the Count answered.

The children had not come down to dinner, but had eaten their supper in the schoolroom which was actually an extremely attractive room with French windows opening onto the garden.

When Linetta had been shown it by the Countess, she had exclaimed at its comfort and attractiveness.

"I expect my husband has told you," the Countess said, "that we were given this house because he would be a better protection for the Prince than if we stayed in what had always been the house for the Secretary of State for Foreign Affairs."

"This is delightful!" Linetta exclaimed.

"Yes, I know," the Countess agreed. "The house we should have had was small and rather dark. Although it was nearer to the Houses of Parliament, it was certainly not particularly attractive."

She smiled as she said,

"You can easily understand how pleased I was to have this house which belonged to His Royal Highness's mother. The children love the garden as I am sure that you will too."

"It is so beautiful," Linetta replied.

Later she was even more delighted when she found that there was a music room in the house and it was far better equipped than she had expected.

There was a large up to date piano besides other instruments like a violin, a harp and a trumpet.

Apparently the previous owner had her own private band and all their instruments had been left where they had always been including many sheets of music.

Linetta thought it would be wonderful to play with the windows open, looking onto the flower-filled garden, which would be an inspiration in itself.

It was when dinner was finished that the Count said very kindly,

"I am sure, Miss Lane, that you are very tired after such a long journey and would like to retire to bed."

He smiled as he continued,

"I had thought of asking you to play to my wife as I know that she is longing to hear the beautiful music you will teach the children, but it would be cruel not to let you rest tonight, while tomorrow we might sing a very different tune."

Linetta laughed.

"You are very considerate and thank you, I would like to go to bed now as I am sure that there is much for me to explore tomorrow."

"Much, indeed," the Count replied.

Linetta then curtseyed to both the Countess and the Count and left the room.

Upstairs in her bedroom that also overlooked the garden, she stood for a long time at the window wondering whether one day she would be in the garden next door, perhaps in charge of The Palace itself.

'If he is as charming and attractive as the house he lives in,' she thought, 'then it will not be difficult for me to stay. But he may, in point of fact, be different.'

She had thought while she was driving through the streets to The Palace that the people themselves were on the whole good-looking and striking.

Equally there were men who perhaps were Russians and their faces were rather frightening.

They looked at the carriage they were travelling in with what she thought was an unpleasant expression in their eyes.

Quite suddenly she was somehow apprehensive and longed to be back in England with her beloved father and mother.

'I am so alone here,' she told herself.

She felt herself tremble.

She had a sudden wish to run away to hide and then rush back to her own home to be with those she loved.

Yet here she was in a strange and intimidating place with the Russians at their gates and the people themselves incapable of keeping them away.

'I want to come home, Papa,' she said silently to herself. 'Why did I listen when they scared me by saying that these people, who are nothing at all to do with us, might be conquered by the Russians?'

It was then she knew that she wanted to run away.

To go back home to the comfort and security that she had always known in England.

To forget Samosia and the threats of the Russians upon people she had never seen before.

They might, for all she knew, be quite content to allow the Russians to order them about, rather than their Prince whom she had not yet met.

She had tried not to think about him while she was travelling through the Mediterranean and past the Greek Islands to where she was now.

'Of course,' she thought to herself, 'what I have always wanted is the love that Apollo, as the King of Love, offers to those who worship him.'

The very love that she realised now she might never find with the man she was marrying to save him and his people from the Russian yoke.

'Why did I ever agree to anything so crazy?' she asked herself.

Then she felt that the Count has been very clever in making her believe how many people might be killed and those who survived might be terrified and treated cruelly and abominably by their conqueror.

Linetta gazed up at the moon.

'I want to go home,' she told it. 'I am frightened of being here and frightened of what lies ahead of me. Oh, please, please help me to be free as I have always been in the past.'

As the moon shone down on the garden, turning the water and everything around it to silver, the stars seemed to look at her with piercing eyes not of fear, nor danger, but of love.

Linetta found herself thinking that God would not have let her come here if he had not believed that there was something very important for her to achieve.

She had a key part to play in the danger that was waiting just outside the country itself.

It could be controlled only if she did as the stars themselves wanted and brought love, peace and happiness to Samosia.

It was then Linetta turned away from the window and started to undress.

When she had done so, she crept into the large four-poster bed, which was in itself very lovely and she felt as if its arms enfolded her.

It was strangely almost as comforting as her father or mother would have been.

'You are never alone,' the stars seemed to tell her. 'We are with you. We and the angels are looking after you and protecting you. You must not be afraid to hold your head high and to pray that if you are scared of the Russians then they are more scared of the British.'

Linetta could hear these words as clearly as if they had been said aloud.

They were coming to her just like the soft sound of music.

It was a tune that she felt she must play to herself tomorrow.

It was a tune that she had never heard before.

Yet somehow she realised in a flash that it was of great significance to her.

She did not know why.

She just knew that it was there in her mind and her head.

For the moment she could not escape from it.

A tune in fact that made what was happening not frightening but magical, a tune which she knew in some strange way spoke to her of love.

CHAPTER FIVE

Prince Ivor, having spent the night with his friends who lived by the sea, then said goodbye to them rather reluctantly.

He knew when he returned to his Palace that there would be a large number of problems waiting for him that his people would insist that he solve for them even though they were insoluble.

He thought as well that there would be an endless number of complaints against the Russian infiltrators who were already secreted inside the City and those who were still determined to force their way in however much those on guard tried to prevent them from doing so.

"I wish I could stay with you for at least a week," he told his host who chuckled.

"There is always a room for you here, Your Royal Highness, and you know we love having you with us," was the reply.

The Prince thought for a moment that perhaps he would stay a little longer just to enjoy himself as he had been so relaxed with his good friends.

But, because he had been brought up by his father and by all those who served him to put duty first, he knew that he must return speedily to the City.

"Goodbye and thank you so much again," he called out as he rode off.

His escort was keeping well behind as he disliked them intruding on him or riding beside him.

It was when he was moving swiftly across the open land and birds that had been nestling in the long grass were flying up in front of him, he suddenly remembered that by now his Secretary of State for Foreign Affairs should have returned from England.

As the Prince knew only too well, he had gone to see Queen Victoria to beg her, if necessary on his knees, to send them a Princess to save his precious country from the Russian invasion.

He was only too well aware that it was only the Union Jack that could save him.

The Russians were becoming ever more outrageous every day and more of them were creeping into the City however hard the Samosian Army tried to stop them from doing so.

As he rode on, the Prince was thinking that the last thing he wanted was a dull English bride.

If it had been a case of taking a Frenchwoman as his wife, he knew that, however difficult she might be, she would still be amusing.

Her wit would keep him laughing even when things were at their most serious.

Alternatively he had always had a special affection for the Greeks.

When he was quite young, he thought perhaps if he was lucky that he would find someone who resembled one of the Greek Goddesses themselves.

She would keep him in love with her because she was so beautiful and because she understood love as only the Greeks seemed to be able to do.

But it had been inevitable when he had watched the Princes in the other Principalities either topple completely in front of the Russian invasion or, if they were fortunate, be provided with an English wife who made the Russians turn round and return in haste to their own country rather than face British retribution.

'I expect the Count has managed to find someone for me,' he thought as he rode on.

He was passing through the part of the country that he most admired.

The rivers, wide and silver, rushed past as they coursed towards the sea.

Every so often a stork rose from the riverside to fly high up into the mountains that still held a touch of the snow that had covered them in the winter.

'I love my country,' the Prince thought to himself as he rode on.

At the same time it was demanding a sacrifice from him that he found hard to meet.

He had always imagined that one day he would be married.

His sons would learn how to ride from him, how to shoot and how to rule the people of Samosia in the same brilliant and outstanding way that their ancestors had done over the centuries.

For his daughters he felt that it would be easy to find them handsome and enterprising husbands, who would make them happy.

Their families would certainly make the Balkans more charming and delightful than they were already.

'That is the life I want,' he said to himself, as he pushed his horse forward.

Then suddenly he felt that he must return quickly to the City in case anything had gone wrong whilst he had been staying with his friends.

Not that something went wrong every day.

But he thought when he retired to bed at night that his problems and worries were increasing.

At the same time if only Queen Victoria would give him her blessing he knew that the Russians would then withdraw.

And Samosia could then go back to being the quiet, happy and contented country it had been since his father's time.

'Why is this happening to me?' he asked himself again.

It was the same question that had been asked many times before.

The Palace was now just ahead of him.

He thought as he had thought so often that it was extremely attractive and romantic.

'If only I had the time,' he mused, 'to choose the woman I want to marry. To love her with the love that has always eluded me and to have children who were the result of our loving each other, how marvellous everything would be.'

Then he told himself with a cynical laugh that he was asking far too much.

He would have to be content if his English bride was good-tempered, demure and obeyed him in things that appertained to the country and if she gave him an heir who would follow him when, like his father, he died.

'I am still asking far too much,' he told himself. 'I must try to give anyone who has come from the Queen my admiration and respect even if I cannot love her, as I would want to do.'

Now he was nearing The Palace and climbing up the hill towards the gates.

He jumped off his horse at a side door where two sentries presented arms.

His butler was waiting for him.

"What has happened while I have been away?" he enquired.

"Nothing very sensational, Your Royal Highness," the butler replied to him. "But the Count has returned from England and, of course, will be anxious to see Your Royal Highness as soon as you have the time."

The Prince took off his riding jacket and gloves and gave them to the butler.

"I will come and see him now," he said. "Tell my secretaries I will be with them as soon as I have seen the Count."

The butler bowed.

The Prince then walked into the garden.

He proceeded towards the house where the Count lived without hurrying himself.

He loved the house, as his mother had, the green lawns, the flowers, the trees and the sun shining on the lake and turning it to silver.

It suddenly struck him that it would be an agony beyond words if he had to leave The Palace.

And to be forced to leave his own country for ever.

There were already a number of Balkan Princes in exile.

Some of them wrote him pathetic letters asking for news of what was happening in their Principality now that the Russians were in charge.

They were undoubtedly, as he was all too aware, extremely homesick.

'I must never be like that,' he reflected, 'however boring and difficult my English bride will turn out to be, I must endeavour to make her happy.'

And because he had loved his mother so deeply, the Prince had made the house she moved into when she had became a widow as beautiful as his Palace.

At times he thought that it was even lovelier and more welcoming.

Certainly the colours of the curtains and the covers of the furniture were all of the soft rose-pink that was her favourite colour.

The carpets bore a touch of rose-pink too while he had chosen for her some of the best pictures that had in the past always been in The Palace.

There was no barrier between The Palace and the house where his mother had lived and died.

As he was walking on increasingly slowly because he was anticipating what he would hear from the Count, he suddenly realised that there was the sound of music coming from the music room of the Count's house.

As music was something he had always loved and this was particularly enchanting, he stood very still for a moment.

He thought that he had never before heard the piano played so brilliantly.

Nor had he heard music that seemed to enter into his very heart.

As it was so entrancing, it was some time before he asked himself who it could possibly be.

How could the Count have found anyone to play in such a marvellous and sublime way?

The Prince must have stood there listening outside the house for over ten minutes.

Then, because he was so curious as to who was the player, he passed quickly on and in through the door that led into a large hall.

On the other side of it was the main entrance.

As soon as he appeared, a man, who was one of the assistants to the Count, hurried forward to say as he bowed deeply,

"Good afternoon, Your Royal Highness. We were hoping that you would return today as no one seemed to be aware of Your Royal Highness's movements."

"Well, I am here," the Prince said, "and I wish to speak with the Count."

"If you will come this way, Your Royal Highness, he is in his private sitting room."

"I know the way," the Prince replied. "There is no need for you to accompany me."

He knew only too well as he spoke that he was familiar with every inch of this lovely house.

It always pleased him that, when it had been given to the Secretary of State for Foreign Affairs, there were very few alterations made.

The house was almost exactly as it had been in his mother's time.

There appeared no one else about, so he opened the door of the sitting room and went in.

The Count was sitting at his writing desk and then looked round to see who had entered.

He sprang to his feet.

"You are now back, thank goodness!" the Prince exclaimed. "I was worrying that too many things might happen before you could return and I only hope that you have brought good news with you."

"Very good news, indeed, Your Royal Highness," the Count replied. "But we will have to wait a short time, perhaps two or three days, before Her Majesty the Queen answers our request completely."

He saw that the Prince was looking worried and added,

"I remain almost certain, Your Royal Highness, that it will be exactly what we want. But naturally I only had a short time with Earl Granville and he had to discuss the matter with the Queen."

"I can understand that," the Prince said. "The only thing that matters is your journey was not in vain."

"I think there is no doubt that Your Royal Highness will be pleased when we hear definitely that the Queen will give us her blessing and provide you with a bride, who will most assuredly be entitled to add the Union Jack to our own flag."

"That is all I want to hear, Count. You have done really splendidly in what I was terrified might be a useless and hopeless visit."

"I was very nervous myself, Your Royal Highness," the Count told him. "But I feel sure that with God's help everything will work out perfectly."

The Prince was smiling.

Then he said,

"I was hearing the most beautiful music when I was walking along outside the house just now. So beautiful that I just could not believe it was actually emanating from the window of your music room. Who can it possibly be and how could you have found someone who could play the piano so sublimely?"

"Do come and meet her for yourself, Your Royal Highness," the Count suggested. "I think that you will be as surprised as I was. Actually she has come here out of the kindness of her heart to teach my children to play the piano."

"If they can learn to play like that then they will be known all over the world," the Prince commented.

Smiling secretly to himself as this was exactly what he would like, the Count walked ahead to open the door for the Prince to pass through.

Then he led him down the passage in the direction of the music room.

Just before they reached it, the Count stopped and said,

"I know that Your Royal Highness will excuse me, but someone is calling shortly with an important message and I must be there to receive it."

He paused before he added,

"Your Royal Highness knows the way to the music room and do introduce yourself as I am sure that the player will be very honoured by your appreciation."

He did not wait for the Prince to reply, but hurried away as if he was feeling concerned that he might miss the messenger.

The Prince put his hand on the door handle.

Then he listened for a few moments to hear again the exquisite notes of music that he knew was something he had never heard in his whole life.

He could only imagine that it was music that came from Heaven itself.

He opened the door.

Sitting at the piano with her back to him was a girl with a glorious head of golden hair that shone brightly in the sunshine streaming in through the window.

The Prince stood there listening, his heart singing at the extraordinary notes coming from the piano.

Then, as she came to what must have been the end of the piece she was playing, Linetta ran her fingers up and down the keys.

She rose intending to walk to the window.

As she did so, she realised that there was someone else in the room.

She turned round and saw that it was an extremely handsome young man.

He had dark hair and was taller than average.

He was wearing riding clothes and looked so smart that he could have just stepped out of a fashion magazine.

He moved towards her with the lithesome grace of an athlete.

As he reached her, the Prince said,

"How is it possible that you can play the music I have never heard before, but which seemed to me to come from the sunshine and the flowers and not from any human being?"

Linetta laughed.

"That is the nicest compliment I have ever had."

"Allow me to introduce myself," he smiled. "I am Prince Ivor of Samosia and I was coming here to see the Count when I heard you playing such exquisite notes. And who are you, if I may ask?"

"I am Miss Linetta Lane from England," she replied to him, "and I have just arrived, Your Royal Highness, to teach the piano to the Count's three children."

She then sank to the floor in a deep curtsey.

"You must come and play for me," the Prince said. "I have often wanted someone like you in my theatre, but I had no idea that such a brilliant musician existed except in my imagination."

"Your Royal Highness is most complimentary," she replied. "I would love to play in your theatre. I did not know you had one."

"It is not a very large one," the Prince said. "But my father and mother had it put into The Palace when I

91

was young because she wanted to have the Nativity play performed at Christmas and we, of course, wanted to act in it."

He stopped for a moment before he went on,

"Of course our friends were invited to applaud as I would love to invite them to applaud you."

There was silence for a moment.

Then Linetta said,

"May I suggest something, Your Royal Highness?"

"Yes, of course, Miss Lane," he answered.

"I would really like," Linetta began, "to see your theatre and play in it before you invite any guests."

She smiled at him as she continued,

"You will realise that the music I have just been playing is attuned to this room which is not very large. In a theatre I would have to play in a different way so that the tune is heard at its very best in the back row as well as the front."

The Prince laughed.

"I understand exactly what you are saying. I would like to suggest that, if you would come to The Palace after dinner tonight, we will try out the acoustics in my theatre. Then we will decide when and how you can astonish the whole of Samosia with your wonderful talent."

"As Your Royal Highness is so pleased with my playing," Linetta replied, "I would like not only to play to you tonight but to practice in your theatre if you would allow me to do so, before anyone else was there to applaud or perhaps to criticise me."

"I cannot believe anyone would criticise someone who plays as gloriously as you do," the Prince said. "As you say, we must give your music the right setting and, of course, the theatre must be as beautiful as it is possible to make it when such melodies are sweeping through it."

"It sounds very exciting. If Your Royal Highness will tell me what time I am to be in the theatre, I will be there. It would be wise to be certain that the programme we give your friends is perfect."

"That is just what we will do," the Prince agreed. "I would like to ask you to dinner, but if I do so I will have to ask the Count and his wife and doubtless several other Courtiers."

He paused before he went on,

"You know as well as I do that would mean they would talk and talk and it would be difficult for us to get away and listen – not to their voices, but to the music you transmit through your fingers, Miss Lane!"

Linetta laughed.

Then she said,

"That sounds the best possible arrangement, Your Royal Highness, and I will be there if you tell me what time you will be free."

"I feel at this very moment that nothing is more important than that I should listen to you play," he replied. "But, as you doubtless know, I have been away and there is sure to be a mountain of letters and messages for me to attend to."

Linetta smiled.

"Your Royal Highness can be very certain of that."

"Very well," the Prince said. "I will dine early at eight o'clock and meet you at the theatre at nine. No one else will be present to criticise or applaud until we have worked out a programme to please ourselves."

"It will have to be perfect. As I have already told Your Royal Highness, I would very much like to be free to practice in your theatre when no one else was present, not even you!"

"My theatre is yours, whenever you want to enter it. Now, as I must not be late for you at nine o'clock, I am going to do my duty that I admit I always find exceedingly tedious."

Linetta smiled.

Then, as she looked up at him, just for a significant moment neither of them was able to look away.

As if he forced himself to do so, the Prince walked towards the door.

"Please tell the Count when he returns that I will be in my study, Miss Lane, and I hope that he will join me as soon as possible to give me his full account of what did happen on his visit to England."

He was gone before Linetta could find words to answer him or drop another curtsey.

Then she sat down on the piano stool looking at the door he had vanished through, almost as if he was still in the room.

The Prince was certainly very different from what she had expected.

In a way he was younger and more enthusiastic and, she had to admit, more charming.

Yet was he what she wanted?

Was he all that she had dreamt about and who she hoped to fall in love with?

'I don't quite know what I really do feel,' she said to herself a little nervously.

The door opened and she thought for a moment that it was the Prince returning.

Instead it was the Count.

"His Royal Highness did find you?" he asked her with a smile.

"He did," Linetta replied. "And I have arranged to play for him in his theatre this evening."

She thought that the Count looked surprised and so she went on quickly,

"He wants to give a party for his friends so that I can play for them, but I insisted that I must practice first in his theatre – "

She stopped as if she thought he did not understand and added,

"I don't know if it is big or small, if I have to play loudly for those sitting at the back or if the acoustics are wrong, in which case my programme might turn out to be a disaster."

"I am sure it would never be that," the Count said. "But I am delighted that you will have the chance of seeing the Prince alone, which is sometimes very difficult for me to arrange."

"I can appreciate that," Linetta replied. "But at the moment he is thinking only of my music and it would be a great mistake to make him think of anything different that would upset him."

"I know what you are saying," the Count agreed. "But I must tell you that the reports I have been receiving since I returned to Samosia, are very bad and the situation here is now extremely serious."

He spoke quietly almost as if he was afraid that someone might overhear him.

"Do you really still think that the Russians intend to take over the whole country?" Linetta asked him.

"I promise you I am not exaggerating," the Count replied, "when I tell you that every day they are coming closer to marching in and the first victim will undoubtedly be His Royal Highness."

Linetta stared at him and then she asked,

"You don't mean that they will kill or imprison him?"

"Those who have been able to escape," the Count replied, "have only done so by leaving the country before the Russians arrived, not after they were inside it."

Linetta put her hands up to her eyes.

"I cannot believe that this is really happening in the modern world which we think has progressed from all that was primitive, cruel and abominable."

"I agree with you," the Count answered. "But the Russians are determined to find their way to the sea and there is only one person who can prevent them from doing so."

There was silence and then Linetta said,

"You are still asking too much of me. How can I tell you that I can marry a man who I have only spoken a few words to?"

"I understand your difficulty, of course I do," the Count said. "But, if you wait for too long, then we will not only lose our great country and its Ruler, but the freedom of everyone who lives here and have, until now, been a happy and contented nation."

As if she could not bear to listen to him, Linetta walked towards the door.

"I am going to rest before dinner," she said, "as I have to be in the theatre at nine o'clock,"

"I will see that you are not late," the Count replied.

As she disappeared, shutting the door behind her, he put his hand up to his forehead.

He was feeling the tension of this drama which was almost too much to bear.

But there was nothing else he could do, only pray that by some miracle these two young people could come together and save Samosia and its people.

It was just five minutes before nine o'clock when Linetta walked into the theatre of The Palace to find, as she had hoped, that there was no one there.

The candles were lit on the piano which was placed in the centre of the stage instead of in the orchestra pit as she had expected it to be.

'He is certainly making me a star,' she thought as she sat down on the stool.

Then she looked at the theatre itself and found it to be very attractive.

It had been modelled on a theatre that she had seen in Vienna, except that it was very small, but charming and intimate.

But there was the same distinct colouring, the same arrangement of lights and the same attractive ceiling.

She felt that anyone who was at all artistic would find it a perfect place to perform.

It would be easy enough to make her music heard by everyone in the theatre no matter how far away from the stage they were sitting.

As she wanted to know how good the piano was, she ran her fingers tentatively over the keys only to be instantly pleased with the result.

Then, as if she could not help herself, she began to play one of her favourite tunes.

It was one she always felt somehow lifted her up into the sky and that she was playing to the stars rather than to an audience.

Carried away by her own music, Linetta went on playing.

Only when she stopped and dropped her hands into her lap did she hear someone clapping.

She sensed that the Prince had entered silently and had been sitting listening to her.

"It is wonderful, wonderful," he said as he walked up to the stage. "Who could have taught you anything so marvellous?"

It was a question and she paused before she replied to him,

"Actually I composed it myself. When I play this piece, I always feel happy and the difficulties I am facing seem to slip away."

"That is exactly how I feel," the Prince remarked.

For a moment there was silence.

And then he said,

"I am going to sit down again and I would like you to play something to me that will answer the huge number of questions that are besieging me at the moment – "

He hesitated before he went on,

"I just don't know why I have asked you that. But, because I cannot answer them myself, I feel certain that you have been sent down from Heaven to answer them for me."

"I feel that you may be asking too much, Your Royal Highness," Linetta replied, "but I will do my best to help."

The Prince moved as if to go back into the stalls and then changed his mind.

He sat on the stage a little way away from her and watched her face while she was playing.

He was aware that, as soon as she touched the keys, she had almost forgotten his presence.

She was concerned only with her music and what it was saying to her.

He had always believed that the real music could answer the human questions it was presented with.

His mother had told him that it was the voice of angels.

The problems of the world could, and were, solved by the wonder and beauty of music.

Certainly, as he listened to Linetta, he felt as if the difficulties that had confronted him in his sitting room and had followed him into the theatre were moving away.

Instead he was looking at a clear sky and seeking a happiness which he believed was his, if only he could find it.

Only when Linetta's music slipped away so softly that it seemed not just to stop but to vanish did the Prince realise where he was and who he was listening to.

Then, after a long precipitous pause when neither of them spoke or moved, he rose to his feet.

"That was the most beautiful music that I have ever heard, Miss Lane," he said in a deep voice. "What is it called and how can I obtain a copy of it?"

Linetta gave a little laugh.

"That is an impossibility I am afraid, Your Royal Highness."

"An impossibility?"

"It is something that I have never played before," Linetta replied. "It came to me when you asked me to take away your problems or perhaps find an answer to them."

"You mean that you composed it on the spur of the moment?"

She nodded.

"I can hardly believe it," the Prince murmured. "It is the most beautiful music I have ever heard. You told me what I wanted to know and I felt that if I did certain things I would find what I was seeking and that, most of all, is happiness."

"I am glad you felt all that," Linetta said. "It is what I felt too and what I was trying to say to you, Your Royal Highness, but then I could never have done so in words."

"Of course not," he agreed. "There are not words that can answer the questions that come from the heart."

"There is something I want to play to you," Linetta said. "I can feel it accumulating in my mind, so you must listen to it. I am sure that it will tell you exactly what you want to know."

Without answering her, the Prince went down and sat once again by the piano.

Then very very softly Linetta began to play on the piano something that seemed to him so intimate.

It was so much a part of herself that it was almost as if he was talking to her and telling her what he secretly desired more than anything else and what really he longed for.

How long she played, he had no idea.

Then, as her music gradually came to an end and vanished in the same way as it had done before, he gave a deep sigh.

"I am not going to talk about it," he said, "because it might just spoil something that is absolutely perfect and something that has never happened to me before."

He paused before he went on,

"It is enough to say that you have told me what I need to know and what I must do and now it would be too much if you gave me any more to think about."

"I think that we should both retire to bed," Linetta said. "I too am tired and as you know we only arrived yesterday after a very speedy journey from England."

They reached the door and then the Prince suddenly asked her,

"Do you ride, Miss Lane? I have a strong feeling, although I cannot think why, that you are a rider and love horses."

"I would be very thrilled to ride one of your horses that I saw this morning, Your Royal Highness," she said. "I thought that they were all magnificent."

"Then we will ride tomorrow morning," the Prince suggested, "but alone, because I wish to talk to you."

He smiled as he added,

"Although they will disapprove, we will go without an escort and I will show you some of the beauties of my country that I now believe could only be expressed in your ethereal music."

"I would love that," Linetta enthused excitedly.

"If you meet me at six-thirty outside in the garden," the Prince told her, "I will choose a horse that I know you will appreciate and we will then ride alone while everyone else is still sleeping."

"How fantastic," Linetta murmured.

The Prince opened the door for her and she went out of the theatre.

He stopped briefly to turn out the lights before he joined her.

As he closed the door behind him, he realised that she had vanished.

She had disappeared as swiftly as her music had finished.

For a moment he wanted to run after her and stop her.

Then he knew that it would be a mistake.

For a short while they had passed from reality into a world of beauty and perfection and he must not now spoil it.

As he walked slowly up the stairs to his room, he thought that he must be dreaming.

CHAPTER SIX

The sun was shining brightly.

And there was that special exhilarating feeling that the world was coming alive that only comes with the dawn.

Linetta found that her mother had packed a very pretty light blue riding outfit for her.

She put it on thinking that it was exactly what she wanted, as later in the day it would be much hotter than it was at the moment.

As she pushed a blue handkerchief into one of the pockets, she remembered that her father had said to her,

"There is something I am going to give you which I know you will take great care of. You must also use them very carefully."

"What is it, Papa?" Linetta asked him eagerly.

"It is these," he replied.

He held out his hands and she saw that in them were two small pistols.

They were ornamented with a strange pattern which she guessed was Russian.

Years ago her grandmother had shown the pistols to her and had told her that she had been given them when she had visited St. Petersburg.

"There was a man there," she said, "who had the most marvellous designs in precious stones and enamel and these pistols were the very latest by Peter Carl Fabergé and he gave them to me as a present."

"They are really lovely, Grandmama," Linetta had replied, "and far too pretty to be anything as violent and as destructive as pistols."

"That is what I thought myself," her grandmother responded. "But my friend told me very solemnly that I should always carry them with me when I went to strange parts of the world and that was certainly true of Russia at that time."

There was a pause before the old lady had carried on,

"Because my husband insisted, I took them with me everywhere I went and we travelled to a great number of countries. I cannot remember ever using them, but they certainly gave me a sense of protection and a feeling that I could always defend myself if the necessity arose."

"So that is why you are giving them to me, Papa," Linetta asked in a low voice.

"Yes, my dear. I have heard what is happening in the Balkans and those Russians have become much more violent lately than they were when I was young."

"I only hope I will not have to use them," Linetta said. "They are so pretty that they would ornament any table they were displayed on."

"That is what I hope they will do," he replied. "At the same time I think you are sensible enough to know that in any foreign country especially in the Balkans you might have to defend yourself when you least expect it. So do see that these pistols are kept loaded and always carry them with you in your pocket."

Linetta had laughed.

"You are remembering that you taught me so well to shoot with my left hand as well as my right, Papa."

"It is exactly what I always did when I was a boy, although they laughed at me and on one occasion when I was travelling in a foreign country, I was unable to use my right hand, but my left killed a man who was attacking me and that saved my life."

"I have always believed you were an exceptionally good shot, Papa," Linetta said.

Her grandmother had told her that he had received prizes for shooting at his school, although he did not talk about it.

He had been in dangerous places where it was very satisfying to know that he could, if necessary, save his own life and the lives of those who were with him.

Linetta was gazing at the pistols.

Then she said,

"They are very pretty and I really should not take them from you, Papa."

"I will be very hurt if you refuse to," her father answered. "I want you to promise me that, whenever you go out without a proper escort, you will carry them hidden somewhere in your bag or in your pocket so that they are there to defend yourself if there is no one else to do it for you."

Linetta chuckled.

"I feel that where I go will be nice safe places like France and Italy. Nevertheless, Papa, I will take them with me."

"There's a good girl and a sensible one," her father had sighed.

When she was leaving for the Balkans, she thought that her father would certainly insist on her taking the two pistols with her, especially when she was pretending to be a Governess and would not have a special guard to look after her.

Now, as she was riding with the Prince and, as he had said without an escort, her father would most definitely want her to carry them secreted in the pocket of her riding coat.

Fortunately the pockets were deep and by pressing them in sideways Linetta was certain that they were well hidden.

Equally she could feel that if necessary she could protect herself.

'One thing is quite certain,' she thought as she took a last glance in the mirror, 'no one will pay any attention to me if I am with the Prince. I think perhaps it is very risky of him to go riding without an escort.'

Whatever she might think, the garden was looking so beautiful when she went downstairs and walked towards The Palace.

It was impossible to think that anyone would want to fight when they could relax in the glorious sunshine.

The only noise she could hear was that of the bees as they fluttered over the flowers and the birds as they flew up into the olive trees.

There was no one to be seen as she walked up to The Palace.

Instinctively, instead of going to the gate that led into the garden, she walked on towards the stables.

As she anticipated, the Prince was already there.

He was supervising the saddling of the horses that Linetta could see at a glance were unusually fine.

In fact she had to admit to herself that they were as good as any horseflesh that her father owned.

If she was really honest, they were the finest horses she had ever seen.

The one the Prince had obviously chosen for her, which already had a side saddle, was almost white except for a touch of black on its nose and fetlocks.

As she walked towards it, Linetta knew that it was exceptional in every way.

It was a great compliment on the part of the Prince to have chosen such a superb horse for her to ride.

As it was so early in the morning, there were only two men saddling the horses.

She realised that they were just humble employees and they would, therefore, not think it strange, as an older and more influential man might do, for her to be riding alone with the Prince.

"Oh, there you are, Miss Lane," the Prince said, raising his hat as she walked up to him. "I thought that we would set off early before it becomes too hot and our escort is waiting outside for us."

His eyes twinkled and almost winked at her as he spoke.

Linetta knew that he was saying this to reassure the two men who were now pulling in the girths of the two horses.

"This is a very beautiful mare," she said, patting the one he had chosen for her.

"Her name is Angel and I thought that name was particularly appropriate to you," the Prince told her.

He lowered his voice as he said the last words so that only Linetta could hear them.

She looked up at him and smiled.

"Thank you, Your Royal Highness," she said softly.

Then she continued to pat the horse she was to ride and began to talk to it.

Her father had taught her that it was very important to talk to any animal one rode, especially those that were the most outstanding and more intelligent than their stable mates.

Linetta therefore told Angel in a soft voice how beautiful she was.

And also how she was sure that she would enjoy riding her.

The Prince was attending, for the moment, to the horse he was to ride.

When he came back and heard Linetta's soft voice, he remarked,

"I might have known, as you are English, that you would treat your horse as a good friend or should I say a lover."

Linetta laughed.

"I think it would be difficult to find any man as handsome as Angel."

"Because she is carrying you, she should really be an Archangel to appreciate anyone so lovely," the Prince remarked.

Because he spoke in a low voice so that the men concerned with the horses should not hear what he said, Linetta answered in the same way by reposting,

"As I have no wish at the moment to be carried up into Heaven, I am perfectly content to be down here on earth with Angel!"

The Prince grinned and said,

"I might have known you would be able to retort to anything that was said to you. And I should be particularly interested to hear what you say about the place I am taking you to."

"Is it somewhere special, Your Royal Highness?" Linetta enquired.

"It is for me, Miss Lane," the Prince replied.

He realised as he spoke that the horse he was to ride was now ready.

Without asking Linetta, he lifted her up in his arms and set her on Angel's saddle.

As she picked up the reins in her hands, she thought that this was such an exceptional horse that she must tell her father about it and make certain that she did so as soon as he arrived.

It flashed through her mind that he would only be coming if she agreed to marry the Prince.

If she decided not to, she would merely creep away to the Port and leave for England quickly before anyone in The Palace could realise what was going on.

As the Prince flung himself onto the saddle of his horse, they moved away without speaking, past the sentries guarding the gate into the stables almost before they were aware that it was the Prince himself.

As they reached the open land behind The Palace, the Prince urged his horse into a gallop.

Angel followed without any encouragement from Linetta.

Now they were well away from the City and on the open land that Linetta knew finally extended all the way to the sea.

At this stage they were riding along beside a swiftly moving river and on the other side of it was a range of high mountains some of them still topped with snow.

The grass they were riding through was high and, as they moved on through it, scores of butterflies, most of them a deep golden yellow, fluttered out of the grass ahead of them.

It was so beautiful with everything shimmering in the rising sun.

Linetta thought that Angel must have carried her into a very special Heaven which she had never imagined before.

They rode swiftly without speaking for about half a mile.

Then, as the Prince drew in his horse, he smiled at Linetta and declared,

"Now we are well away from everything but our dreams."

It was such a strange remark for him to make that Linetta merely gazed at him.

As if she had asked him a question, he added,

"Where else in the whole wide world would it be possible for me to find anyone as beautiful as you riding on an Angel!"

"Who is, without exception, the most superb horse I have ever seen in my life," Linetta said. "But then yours, Your Royal Highness, is particularly fine as you naturally know."

"He is called Firefly because of his colour," the Prince told her. "He has been my favourite horse for over a year."

He paused for a moment before he continued,

"I have often wondered who would be the perfect person to accompany me on Angel. But I never imagined that my dreams of finding one would come true."

Linetta smiled at his delightful compliments.

And then she said,

"I think that you must still be lost in the music you heard last night, Your Royal Highness. And what is more I am sure that we are still hearing it in our minds."

"I am hearing mine in my heart," the Prince replied. "That is what you aroused in me last night. I was moved as I have never been moved before."

"That is such a lovely thing to say to me," Linetta murmured.

She was thinking as she spoke that just as her father had fallen in love with her mother because her music, he had said, carried him into a world he had never known, in which he found the perfect love that he had dreamt of but thought that he would never find.

Linetta could not help thinking it was very strange, but at the same time wonderful, that the same music which she had learnt from her mother had appealed to the Prince in the same way as it had to her father.

They rode on for a while before the Prince said,

"Because of what I thought last night and in a way I suppose it is something I have felt before, I am now taking you to a place that somehow connects me with your music, you and another world far away from the strife and deceit of this one."

Linetta did not ask him any questions.

She merely glanced at him and he then said, as if she had spoken,

"It is a very special place I go to when I am feeling worried or perplexed and where I have never taken anyone else."

"You are just making me more and more curious, Your Royal Highness," Linetta sighed.

"I think only you would understand what it means to me," the Prince confided. "In fact, when I was thinking about it last night, I thought that what this place means to me is the same as your music means to you."

Linetta could not find an answer to him.

Yet she could not help thinking it was strange that her music had aroused so much in the Prince's imagination that he wished to take her to a place which to him was very private and probably sacred.

It was all very intriguing in its own way.

However, she asked no questions.

They rode on with the butterflies fluttering up in the air again and some of them settled on Linetta's head and Angel's mane.

The sun was rising in the sky, but the dewdrops of the night still glistened on the grass.

When they passed an occasional tree, the birds flew out as if surprised by their intrusion into a world that seemed completely devoid of people.

"I had no idea that your country was so lovely," Linetta said to the Prince.

"Then how could I lose all this to the Russians?" he asked, almost harshly.

"It is something you must not do," she said without thinking.

Then she realised that it was her hand which held the trump card.

Because she was a little apprehensive at what they were doing and at what he had just said, she pressed her horse forward.

Once again they were galloping so swiftly that it was impossible to start a conversation.

They must have travelled for over a mile when she saw ahead that there was a large wood crossing the field from the river into the distance.

It was so far away that she could not see the end of it.

Almost instinctively she then drew Angel into a trot which soon became a walk.

"You must tell me about yourself, Miss Lane," the Prince said to her unexpectedly.

Linetta started as if wakening from a deep sleep and managed to reply,

"I would much rather hear about you, Your Royal Highness."

"What can I say about myself?" the Prince asked. "I have inherited this beautiful land and now it is in danger. A danger that haunts every Prince like myself."

"Then you must not allow the Russians to take it from you, Your Royal Highness," Linetta urged him.

"I expect you know," the Prince replied, "as you are staying with our Secretary of State for Foreign Affairs, that he has asked the Queen of Great Britain to give me the one thing that the Russians fear and that is an English bride. But I have not yet heard from Her Majesty what her answer will be."

Linetta thought that the Count had been very clever in making it possible for her to get to know the Prince without there being any obvious reason why she should do so in such haste.

Or why indeed she was unexpectedly brought from England to teach his children.

Because she was curious, she could not help asking him,

"And, if her Majesty says 'yes', will you not find it very difficult to marry someone you have never met and with whom you will probably have absolutely nothing in common?"

"We will have one thing," the Prince replied, "and that is if she believes, as I most certainly do, that this very beautiful country of Samosia is worth saving."

"Suppose," Linetta said, after a short silence, "she does not please you or you don't please her, what will you do then, Your Royal Highness?"

"It is a question that I have asked myself a million times," the Prince answered. "I suppose like most men I have always wanted to fall in love with someone who will become my wife and to believe that she really loves me for myself and not for my Royal position in the Social world."

He spoke in a way which told Linetta that this was the truth.

She was wondering what to reply when the Prince asked,

"Do you think that it would be easy for me to marry someone under those circumstances, Miss Lane?"

There was silence for a while before he went on,

"Do you think that I would not suffer when I lose the dreams you aroused in me last night that are so much part of me that I felt I should be only half myself without them."

"Perhaps," Linetta suggested, "you will fall in love with the woman the Queen chooses for you."

The Prince laughed and it was not a pleasant sound and then he replied,

"Life is not like that except in our dreams and in your music. Life is cold and harsh!"

There was silence for a moment.

When Linetta did not speak, he carried on,

"Of course I must do everything in my power to make an English bride, if the Queen does give me one, as happy as it is possible for her to be in a strange country with a strange man for whom she obviously has no feeling

113

until she actually arrives and can then see me for the first time."

He spoke grimly and there was now a hard note in his voice.

It told Linetta that he was as apprehensive about the future as she had been before she left England.

"I know without you saying so," the Prince went on, "that you are thinking of an alternative. I have thought and thought and I realise that I have to accept this woman to save my country or refuse her and lose it."

"It may not be as bad as you think," Linetta said softly. "After all she is surely facing the same problem as you are."

The Prince laughed.

"Has there ever been a woman, who has not wanted to marry a King, a Prince, a Duke or a Lord? I will not deceive myself because I would be incredibly stupid to do so."

He gave a sigh as he added bitterly,

"She will marry me just because I am a Prince and doubtless she will make a very good Princess."

As Linetta did not speak, he went on,

"But there will be no room for the dreams such as you awoke in me last night. There will be no answer to the question I want you to pose to the special place where I am taking you."

As if he could not bring himself to say any more, he spurred his horse forward.

Linetta then had some difficulty in catching up with him.

In fact they had almost reached the trees which lay ahead of them, before the Prince pulled up his horse once again to a walk.

"You must forgive me," he said, as Linetta came beside him. "I have lain awake night after night thinking of my future and I am afraid, desperately afraid, that it will never be the same as it has been throughout these past few years."

"Tell me about it," Linetta suggested softly.

"When I came to the throne, as you may say," the Prince began, "I was still dreaming that one day I would have with me someone I loved who would help me bring to my people not riches but happiness. I want Samosia to be a happy country not just a wealthy one."

He paused before he continued,

"And a country where children are born of love and my people as a whole are content to obey me as their Ruler and would therefore make Samosia the most original and outstanding country in the whole of the Balkans."

"Do you really believe that it can happen?" Linetta asked.

"Given the right leadership, given that a man and a woman who will really dedicate themselves not only to the success of the country but the success of each individual in it, I am sure it is possible," the Prince replied. "That is my most important mission."

"In what way?" Linetta enquired.

"In every way. I believe that each one of us has as a present from God, if you like, something that makes us individually unique however poor we might be born."

He stopped for a moment before he went on,

"It is in our minds and in our thoughts. Put those two concepts together and teach the people how to do it and they will find that they have capabilities beyond their greatest dreams."

"Of course you are right," Linetta said positively. "I have always believed it myself. But the leader, whoever he may be, must guide them to develop individually until they become themselves leaders to the next generations."

The Prince smiled.

"Of course that is putting it in even better words than I have managed to do. You do realise that, if I am to make Samosia great and important and the envy of every Principality in the Balkans, I just cannot do it unless I have someone to help me."

He made a gesture with his hands as he asserted,

"And where is she to be found? I can assure you I have visited most of the Courts in Europe and discovered that, on the whole, their young Princesses are dull, stupid and, although it is a word I hate – ignorant."

He spoke almost violently and Linetta said softly,

"Surely they cannot all be as bad as all that, Your Royal Highness."

"No, that was an exaggeration," he replied. "But most of them would not understand what you and I are saying to each other now. Nor would they believe that your music could awaken in those who listen to it all the ambitions that not only Rulers should have but every man should aim to encourage in his own children."

By this time they had reached the trees that they had seen in the distance.

Then the Prince turned to Linetta and said in a very different voice,

"That is what I hoped I could awaken in my own sons when I have them. But you know as well as I do that the chance of my doing so is now high up in the clouds and I should be a fool if I did not face reality."

As he finished speaking, the Prince dismounted.

He tied his horse's bridle to a fence which encircled several of the trees.

Without saying anything more, Linetta dismounted too and tied the bridle of her horse beside his.

She patted her horse before she turned away from it and then realised that the Prince was waiting for her.

Having slipped off her gloves, she put her hand into his.

"Now I have something to show you which is very important to me," the Prince said. "I would like you to know, Miss Lane, that you are the very first person I have brought here since I was a child."

"Is that really true, Your Royal Highness?" Linetta asked.

"Perfectly. I come here early in the morning, but I am not accompanied by anyone else as I am today."

There was a slight pause.

"But because this will remind you of the music you were playing last night," he continued, "just as your music told me I must bring you here because there is an affinity between us that no man could possibly put into words."

As he finished speaking, he drew Linetta forwards.

His fingers closed over hers.

She felt a little quiver running through her, which somehow was different from anything that she had ever felt before.

Then it seemed as if they were entering what was a tunnel of old bricks and ancient trees that had grown up between them.

Just ahead where the trees were thicker and their branches shut out the sunshine, there was what looked to Linetta to be a pool of water in the ground.

It was so unusual and different from anything she had seen before that for a moment she wondered just why it seemed to mean so much to the Prince.

And why he had never, as he said, brought anyone here.

Then before she could ask him any questions, he said very quietly,

"This is an ancient wishing well. It is so old that it was here almost before this country had people living in it and certainly very few houses."

"A wishing well!" she exclaimed. "How exciting, how did you find it, Your Royal Highness?"

"From very antique records that most people would find impossible to read. I had them deciphered by the most brilliant professors in our University."

He sighed before he went on,

"They took a long time before they finally found that it was a wishing well and it had been believed by the people who came to this part of the world to have magical powers if they prayed into it and asked the demons or the fairies to which it belonged for anything they desired."

By this time they were standing looking down into the wishing well.

As the Prince was still holding her hand, Linetta bent forward to gaze as far as she could into the depths of the water in front of her.

She was thinking that the wishing well itself must be very deep when the Prince said,

"I have been coming here frequently ever since I discovered it with all my problems and difficulties. Most I must admit have been ignored, but then some have been answered."

Linetta was listening very intently and he went on,

"Therefore you must pray as I will and I can only hope that your prayer will be answered even if mine is refused."

"That is very generous of you," Linetta answered. "But if you pray for me, then I will pray for you. I will also wish that you will find happiness."

"The happiness that you gave me last night?" the Prince asked. "I think that very unlikely. Look up and you will see why your sublime music told me that I must bring you here."

Linetta looked up which she had not done as she entered.

Now she saw that the tall trees overhead with the sunshine behind them created a strange mystic beauty that was different from anything she had seen before.

Yet in a way she could understand that, just as it aroused something strange within her as it was so lovely and the sunshine seemed to have turned the leaves of the trees to shimmering gold, the wishing well could, in fact, give those who prayed to it what they desired.

Without being aware of it, her fingers tightened on the Prince's hand.

He looked at her with a faint smile on his face as he said very softly,

"Now you understand. Now you know what you gave me and what I am now trying to give to you."

Because in a way it was so moving, Linetta could not find any words to reply to him.

Then suddenly their heads were turned up towards the flickering light of the sun that came through the trees and a harsh voice rang out,

"Here they are!"

Linetta then looked down and realised that standing opposite them on the other side of the wishing well were two men.

It took her a moment to realise that they were in uniform and were very obviously Russians.

As the Prince's fingers now tightened on hers, they were almost painful.

Then she heard him demand of the Russians,

"Who are you and what are you doing here?"

To her astonishment he did not speak in his own language but in German, which she had always understood the Russians used when they were moving about Europe and not in their own country.

"We have been looking for Your Royal Highness," one of the men replied. "And, as we've been so clever in finding you, we'll certainly be rewarded when we tell those who've sent us that your body lies at the bottom of this well from which it can never be recovered."

As he spoke, he pulled a gun from under his arm and the man beside him did the same.

It flashed through Linetta's mind that these men were about to kill the Prince and she felt the full horror of the moment and could only gasp.

Then she remembered the pistols which were in the pocket of her coat.

Swiftly, so swiftly that the two men on the other side of the wishing well were not even aware that she had moved, she pulled out both the pistols.

Even as the man who had spoken brought his gun down towards the Prince's head, she shot him between the eyes.

The other man she then shot in the throat with the pistol in her left hand.

The noise of the gunfire seemed to echo as the men fell backwards.

Then the Prince, who appeared to have been almost in a dream, put his arm around her and drew her away from the wishing well and outside to where their horses were tied.

Only as they reached them, did Linetta manage to stammer in a shaky voice,

"They were going – to kill you."

"You saved my life, my darling," he sighed.

He pulled her into his arms as he spoke.

Then his lips came down on hers and he held her closely against him.

For a second Linetta could hardly believe what was happening.

Then she felt something strange within her heart.

It was a feeling that she had never known before.

Yet it seemed to fill her mind and her body in a way that she did not understand.

But she knew it was something wonderful that she had always hoped to find one day.

The Prince's lips were on hers and his arms were round her so closely that she could hardly breathe.

Without saying a word he picked her up in his arms and put her onto Angel's back.

He set her free and then he just seemed to leap onto his own horse.

Only as he started to move off with Linetta behind him, did he say,

"There are sure to be others with them, they would not be alone. So we must ride as quickly as we can back to civilisation."

He did not wait for her answer, but bent forward to urge his horse into moving even quicker than it had done before and Linetta did the same.

She knew that the Prince was right in thinking that the two Russians would not be alone.

There was perhaps a Regiment of soldiers moving into Samosia with the intention of taking it over, just as in the North of the country there would be another Russian Regiment moving towards the City.

If they had not hurried that much on their way from The Palace, they certainly rode back at a speed that Linetta was to think afterwards was faster than the wind itself.

As they arrived at The Palace gate and the sentries came to attention, they galloped on into the stable yard.

When their sweating horses came to a standstill, the Prince said,

"I must warn the General in Command immediately as well as the Prime Minister of what I am now certain are the beginnings of an invasion by the Russians. Please tell the Count at once what has happened."

It was an order.

Linetta then ran as quickly as she could through the garden until she reached the Count's house.

As she expected, the family were having breakfast.

When she saw them in the breakfast room, she then entered through the French window, which like the others in the house, opened into the garden.

The Count, who was sitting at the end of the table with his children on either side of him, looked up in great surprise as she came bursting into the room.

"What has happened?" he asked anxiously.

"The Russians are closing in on the City," Linetta said breathlessly. "They are coming from the South and the North. Will you tell the Prime Minister that His Royal Highness is doing everything that he can, but you have a special message from Her Majesty the Queen."

"A special message?" the Count managed to say.

He had risen to his feet as Linetta was speaking.

He was staring at her as if he could hardly believe what was occurring.

"What you have to do," Linetta urged, "is to get the Church bells ringing and send out the Heralds – as many as possible – to tell the people of Samosia that Her Majesty the Queen of Great Britain is sending the Prince a bride!"

"So you have now made up your mind," the Count managed to utter.

In his surprise his words seemed to topple over themselves.

"Yes, I will marry the Prince this afternoon at four o'clock," Linetta told him, "and that will be more effective in stopping the Russians than any soldiers could be."

"*This afternoon*!" the Count exclaimed loudly as if he could not have heard her right.

"I am going now to meet my mother and father, who I am certain will have arrived at the Port by now," Linetta answered. "I will need a fast carriage to bring them back in."

"I sent one yesterday," the Count replied, "thinking it might be wanted, but then I was not expecting anything like this."

"There is no time to tell you all about it," Linetta said. "You must send an escort to meet us, as we will go straight to the Cathedral where all the bells must be ringing to welcome us."

She paused before she went on excitedly,

"I want my bridesmaids to be there waiting too and they are to be chosen by your daughters who should be in charge. I want ten of them, as young as possible wearing white dresses with a wreath of pink roses and a bouquet of the same colour roses."

"That will be better than anything the Russians can think of!" the Count cried.

"I want bands to be playing in the streets," Linetta continued, "and a special band will drive in front of us after we are married and on our way back to The Palace."

The Count squared his shoulders.

"I will see to it all immediately," he said.

Linetta turned back, as if to leave the same way she had come.

Then she said,

"I have just thought of something most important. Announce to the people of Samosia that it is the Queen of Great Britain who desires this and must be obeyed that the Prince and Princess are to be crowned immediately their marriage has taken place."

She paused before she added quickly,

"It will be much more difficult for the Russians to fight a King and Queen than a Prince and Princess."

Without waiting for an answer she had gone.

The Count knew that she was running towards his own stable where there were not only horses she could ride but soldiers who guarded The Palace.

She could easily find four men to take her to the Port in safety.

The Count did not follow her.

He looked towards his wife who had been staring at Linetta with amazement.

"Come along, my dearest," he said. "We have our orders. You must help me, as we have little time to carry them out."

He reached the door by the time he had finished speaking and then his wife asked,

"Can you arrange for them married in such a short time?"

The Count smiled.

"To hear is to obey," he said. "God be thanked that she has made up her mind to marry him so quickly."

CHAPTER SEVEN

Linetta reached the stables.

Shortly after she had given the order four soldiers were ready to escort her to the Port.

As they were soldiers, she spoke to the Officer in Command and found that he was of high rank.

She informed him that the Russians were gathering in the South of the country and also, she suspected, in the North.

"The one thing that is important," she said, "is that the Prince should be guarded every moment of the day. From what I hear they are determined to kill him before he can be married."

The Officer was astonished that Linetta knew so much.

At the same time he was wise enough to know that he must follow her instructions.

"I will send a company of men immediately to The Palace," he offered.

"And," Linetta added, "when the English party who have arrived get near to the City, there must be a Company of picked men to protect them until they can reach the Cathedral."

She paused before she went on,

"I am quite certain that the Russians, if they get the chance, will make one last desperate effort to prevent the marriage taking place."

"I understand," the Officer answered. "I can only hope that the lady, who the Queen of Great Britain has sent us, will not be frightened."

Linetta smiled to herself as she replied,

"I am sure that she will be as brave as the English always are when they are in difficulties."

She did not wait for the Officer to respond, but mounted the horse that was now ready for her with a side saddle.

The four soldiers who were to accompany her were already on either side of her and the Officer helped her into the saddle.

She thanked him, feeling sure that he would carry out all her instructions.

Because she was English they would consider them important even though at this very moment she was only a Governess to the three children of the Secretary of State for Foreign Affairs.

She felt sure, however, that the Count would carry out all her requests.

She gave her orders with such an air of authority that she even surprised herself.

And she knew that the children would be thrilled at the idea of being her bridesmaids.

They set off at a very fast pace, so fast that Linetta could not help wondering if they would be able to keep it up all the way to the Port.

It was just over half-an-hour later when the soldier galloping beside her suddenly drew in his horse.

"What is it?" she asked him anxiously.

"There is something beyond that hill," he replied. "It would be a mistake, as we cannot see what is on the other side of it, to rush on without making some sort of investigation."

There were some fir trees not far away from where they were.

Although it was by no means a wood, it was at the least some protection and there were sufficient bushes for them not to be seen.

Three of the soldiers and Linetta then rode under the trees.

The fourth soldier jumped down from his horse.

And going out to the field through which they had just come, he began to move towards the hill almost bent double so that the high grass, some of it in flower with the butterflies fluttering above it, made it difficult for him to be seen.

Waiting for him under the trees and being careful to ensure that their horses were completely hidden, the three soldiers watched in silence as he next went down on his knees as he neared the top of the hill.

As they had a quick glance of him reaching the top, he disappeared.

They waited breathlessly in silence.

Linetta's heart was beating fearfully in case they would be prevented from reaching her father and mother waiting at the Port.

She was also concerned that the soldier might be noticed, as if there were indeed Russians on the other side, he could be accused of spying on them.

And they might kill him or perhaps torture him to give them information about the City and whether it was really intended, as they had heard, that the Prince was to marry a bride from Great Britain.

Linetta was well aware, although she did not put it into words, that if they could kill the Prince before he was married, then it would be very hard to find someone to take his place, someone who would undoubtedly have to fight violently to prevent the country falling into the Russians' hands.

Also it would be highly unlikely that anyone would be willing to take on such a precarious post.

Then at last they were aware that the soldier who was investigating the hill was returning to them, although they only caught a brief glimpse of him moving in the high grass, they realised without being told that something was wrong.

When he reached them, he moved so swiftly into the cover of the bushes that they sensed danger.

"It's the Russians," he managed to say at last in a low voice. "There's at least thirty or forty of them. All, I should imagine, making for the City, unless of course, they are watching the ships for some reason or another."

Linetta felt herself tremble at the thought of them not only stopping her father and mother from helping to save the Prince, but perhaps slaughtering them before they even reached the City.

"What shall we do?" one soldier asked.

"I've no idea," the other replied. "It'd be a mistake for them to see us."

Suddenly there was a trumpet call which seemed to echo round and round.

The four soldiers and Linetta stiffened.

Then unexpectedly they could see quite a number of men climbing to the top of the hill.

'They are going straight to the City,' Linetta told herself. 'Perhaps, although I have warned them, they will not protect the Prince and he will be killed.'

She so wanted to warn him and to save him from the Russians.

But she realised that she would be seen if she tried to turn back.

It would be a grave mistake to let her father and mother become involved in what would undoubtedly be a very vicious war.

'What can I do? What can I do?' she asked herself despairingly.

Then one of the soldiers gave an exclamation,

"They're being lined up! It seems very strange, but some of them are facing the other way!"

Linetta was thinking it must be where the Russian Officers were who were giving them orders.

But she only saw the men on top of the hill.

Even so she realised that they were fully armed and in their Russian Army uniforms they looked exceedingly threatening.

It was these men, she thought, who must be the comrades of the two men she had killed at the wishing well.

Perhaps a spy had found out that the Prince often visited the wishing well and they had therefore been told to see if he was there and to kill him.

It would be, as she well knew, a tremendous feather in Russia's cap if they could prevent the marriage, which had the blessing of Queen Victoria, taking place, at the same time removing the rightful Prince whose family had served Samosia for many centuries.

"I cannot think what they are doing," the soldier nearest to Linetta murmured.

Then suddenly there came another blast of trumpets giving the orders to march.

It was then that all the Russian soldiers on the hill looked North as if trying to see the City in the distance.

But now, to Linetta's surprise, they turned left.

As they moved on, she could see clearly the heads of the other men below them and knew that they were on the march too.

They were heading for the wishing well where she had been this morning with the Prince.

It flashed through her mind that they were going in that direction because they had either found or would find the two men she herself had shot.

'They are looking for them,' she thought to herself 'and when they find them, as they will eventually, it will be impossible for them to know whether or not they have been shot by the Prince they were seeking or indeed by someone else.'

She hesitated and then added to herself,

'Perhaps they are seeking the other soldiers who had come down from the Barracks, which like The Palace, is some distance to the right of where they are heading.'

If they were marching, perhaps there would be no real reason for them to hurry, she thought.

They would therefore not reach the wishing well for an hour or more.

If they did return immediately, she was sure by that time that her father and mother would have left the ship and would be on their way to the City.

"They are going away!" the soldier next to Linetta exclaimed. "I wonder where they are going. I expected them to march to the City straightaway, which we have just left and stir things up even more than they are already."

"Well, one blessing is that they will not bother us," the other soldier said. "When we leave this lady with the ship she is expecting from England, we had better get back as quickly as we can and warn them that these new soldiers have just come here by sea and because they are up to no good, the sooner they are sent back to where they have come from the better."

"There we agree with you," the first soldier said. "But we must drop this lady first as we were ordered to do."

"Of course we must," another agreed. "At the same time it is no use her walking into a hornets nest, as one might say, and we had best ride a bit to the left before we turn down the coast towards the Port."

They all concurred with him.

Linetta said a little prayer of thankfulness as they rode out to the left side of the hill.

Looking back she could see that there was no one on the hillside any longer.

She was only very grateful that she had been saved from running into the Russians.

They were clearly on the wrong track if they were intending to kill the Prince before he was married.

'I have certainly been lucky today,' she thought, 'if at no other time.'

If she had not killed the two men who were out to shoot the Prince, then there would be no question of her marrying him to save his country.

She knew now that she wanted to save him more than she had ever wanted anything in her whole life.

She wanted to marry him.

She wanted to be his wife.

She wanted to feel that strange wonderful feeling within her when he kissed her again.

'I love him, I love him!' she said to herself. 'This is the real love that Papa had for Mama. They have never regretted for one single moment leaving London and living in obscurity in Devon with only us children to talk to.'

She had never heard them complain and never felt that they wished for any other life than the one they loved so much together.

'Just how could anyone,' she asked herself, 'want anything more than real love, a love that is so beautiful and so perfect that there is no need for anything else in the world.'

It was a blessing that she had begun to think she might never find for herself.

Yet she wanted it so much because the whole house she lived in had been filled with the love that her father had for her mother and her mother had for her father.

'Is it really possible that I could feel the same?' she asked herself and at once knew the answer.

She had known it almost before the Prince had kissed her.

When his lips had touched hers and she had felt a sudden fervour within her heart, she had known that this was what she had longed for and what she had prayed for, not only occasionally but night after night.

Now so unexpectedly, in fact, it seemed almost a miracle, that in carrying out the wishes of Her Majesty the Queen and being prepared to marry a man she had never heard of, let alone seen before Earl Granville came to their home, she had found the one man who could make her dreams come true.

'I am lucky, extremely lucky,' she thought as they rode on. 'All I have to do now is to help the man I love and keep his country from being overrun and destroyed by those terrible Russians.'

It was a task she thought might petrify almost any woman.

But now, instead of being very frightened, she felt a deep inward happiness that was almost indescribable.

She knew that because of it she would concentrate her mind, her body and her soul in doing what her husband wanted.

And that meant making absolutely certain that this Principality of Samosia in the Balkans was saved from the Russian menace.

'Thank You, God! Oh, thank You so very much!' she said under her breath, looking up at the sky.

She was sure that her prayers reached God and the angels surrounding Him.

They and the Archangels would help her too.

She knew that in the future she could help educate and lead the women of Samosia into a world that they had never known before.

She would make it so wonderful for them that in the years to come they would bless her because she had given them what she had found herself, which was love, the pure undiluted love that all women dream about.

Because she was thinking so much while they were riding she was surprised when they reached the Port even sooner than she had anticipated.

It was then that she began to feel afraid in case the ship from England had not yet arrived.

Because her father had told her so much about his travels she knew that it would be a mistake to go looking for the ship herself.

Instead she went straight to enquire of the Officer in charge of the Port if a ship from England had arrived.

"I have come from The Palace," she told him, "and His Royal Highness requires the occupants of the ship to come to him as soon as possible."

"I understand," the Officer replied, "and I know that you will be glad to hear that the ship came into Port late last night. You may walk to it now and board it."

"That is very kind of you," Linetta said.

Because she looked so lovely, at the same time far more important than he thought her to be, the Officer took her himself down a passage which was a far quicker way of reaching the ship at the quay than going the way usually used by travellers.

When she saw the imposing British Battleship just below her, Linetta wanted to cry out with delight at the sight of it.

Then she guessed that the Queen herself, or more likely Earl Granville, had chosen a Battleship just in case they had to escape quickly from the Russians.

They might have to fight their way to freedom.

Thanking the Officer politely for bringing her to the Battleship, she ran up the gangway.

She found her father and mother on deck and they rushed towards her in excitement when they saw her.

"We did not expect to see you quite so early, my dearest," her father exclaimed in delight, as she kissed him affectionately.

"You will need every available moment when I tell you just what I have planned for you, Papa," his daughter answered.

She sat down opposite them on a deckchair.

As a Steward hurried to fetch her some scrambled eggs to eat and some coffee to drink, she told them that she was being married at four o'clock that afternoon.

And that the sooner they were ready to drive to the City the safer it would be for them and for Prince Ivor.

To make them appreciate the urgency of the current situation in Samosia, she told them a little of what had happened earlier in the day.

Whilst her mother gave a cry of horror, her father merely said,

"It is a miracle that I taught you to shoot with both hands. I will always be eternally grateful to those pistols that belonged to my mother."

"They most certainly saved the Prince's life and mine," Linetta told him. "But I am afraid that the Russians might try a last desperate effort to prevent the marriage taking place."

Her mother gave another cry of horror.

"How can we be ready in that time?" she asked. "I have brought you a wedding dress, but do you really intend to wear it to travel in?"

"I will certainly not be able to change at The Palace before we go to the Cathedral," Linetta answered.

She hesitated for a moment before adding,

"I think I must tell you, Papa, that I have told the Count to inform everybody that it is Her Majesty's wish that we should be crowned as soon as the Wedding Service is completed."

"Crowned!" her father exclaimed. "I feel sure that Her Majesty never said such a thing."

"She is not likely to deny it when she knows that it will save the Prince's life and his country more effectively than if we are to reign over Samosia as mere Prince and Princess."

She paused for a moment before she went on,

"You know just as well as I do, Papa, that for the Russians to kill a relative of Her Majesty is bad enough, but if they should be King and Queen there is no doubt that the English would go to war."

"Perhaps you are right," Prince Vladimir said, "but it would be very unfortunate if Her Majesty should say that she never gave such an order."

"How could she do that and let the Russians back into Samosia?" Linetta asked.

Her father laughed.

"I can see you have an answer to every question and I can only imagine, my dearest, that you will make an excellent Queen, although a somewhat bossy one!"

Linetta grinned.

"Mama has taught me ever since I can remember that you are the Head of the Family and so you are always right."

"Of course he is," her mother agreed. "That is why we are so happy together. I find it much easier to let him have his own way than to argue about it!"

She smiled at her husband as she spoke.

He bent forward and kissed her on the cheek.

"I love and adore you," he said, "and, if Linetta is going to be as happy as we are, then she will be a very lucky girl."

Linetta did not say anything more, she only smiled at her parents.

Then she hurried below decks with her mother to the Master cabin.

"I bought you everything that I could, my darling," she said. "Even though your father would not allow me much time in France, I snatched everything I thought might come in useful."

Actually Linetta was delighted with all the clothes that her mother had brought her.

She realised that they would undoubtedly dazzle the eyes of every woman in Samosia.

There was that touch of *chic* about them that only the French could give to the clothes they designed.

Because she was as clever in her own way as her husband was in his, she had bought a selection of the most entrancing hats for her daughter.

There were pretty underclothes and nightgowns that seemed almost transparent.

At the same time with very little embroidery they were pieces of art that no other country could produce.

"Thank you! Thank you so much, Mama!" Linetta exclaimed. "They are all simply lovely. But please pack them up again as quickly as you can."

A note of fear suddenly came back into her voice as she urged her parents,

"We must go. I am so afraid that the Russians will make a last effort to kill the Prince. If they do, the City and the whole country will be theirs."

Her mother hurriedly packed the clothes back into the boxes she had brought with her.

Then she carefully lifted up the wedding dress from another box.

It was, Linetta thought, exactly the wedding dress she really wanted.

It would definitely leave the women of Samosia gasping when they saw it.

It was made of the softest white chiffon.

Almost as if she had been clairvoyant when she had told the bridesmaids to wear white dresses and carry pink roses, there was just a hint of pink in her wedding dress.

Linetta felt that it was just like a touch of sunshine seeping through the mystery of the wishing well.

Her mother had also brought the family jewels with her.

The tiara was an exquisite piece of work that Prince Vladimir had inherited from his mother and it had been handed down by the family for endless generations.

There was a beautiful necklace to go with the tiara and bracelets for Linetta's wrists.

She knew that she would be shining in the lights from the candles on the altar and in the sunshine when she and her husband drove back to The Palace.

'It will make him think of my music,' she thought to herself.

She knew that she would be inspired to play new tunes that not even her mother and father would have heard before.

She was dressed and ready sooner than her father expected.

But he insisted on them all having a meal before they set out for the City.

"No one can ever be particularly brave on an empty stomach," he said. "Therefore, as we all have to be very brave today, I can only pray that it will not be as bad as we anticipate."

They ate an excellent but very hurried luncheon and Linetta finally put on her beautiful wedding dress.

Then they left the Battleship to get into the carriage that was waiting for them on the quay.

They had not gone far when, to Linetta's delight she saw the soldiers she had asked to meet them marching down the hill towards the sea.

There was a great deal of saluting and shaking of hands and congratulations from the Officer in charge.

Because Linetta did not want them to recognise her, she pulled the veil of her wedding dress over her face.

Also, as they were in a closed carriage, it would be more difficult for them to have more than a quick glance at her when they welcomed her father and mother.

The Officer in Charge, then thinking that she was just the daughter of Prince Vladimir and not seeing her in the carriage, made an elegant speech of welcome to which she bowed her head.

She murmured her appreciation as if she was very shy.

Then they set off again, but this time much slower than Linetta had travelled on her way to the Port.

At last after quite a long time in the carriage, they saw ahead of them the tall spires of the Churches and the towers of The Palace.

It was exactly a quarter to four.

Linetta felt a wave of excitement rising within her.

Now she would not only see the Prince again but marry him!

She had known when he kissed her that he was the man who had been in her dreams, but who she thought she would never meet in real life.

It was difficult for her to explain, even to herself, what she felt.

But she knew when his lips met hers that her whole body, as well as her heart, responded passionately to him.

This was love, but very much more exciting and marvellous than she had ever imagined it to be.

As they entered the City and their carriage rode on towards the Cathedral, she felt that he had been as moved by the kiss as she had been.

She had known then that she must marry him.

Not just because in doing so she would save the people of Samosia from the dreaded Russians, but because she herself wanted to belong to the Prince.

She found herself, as they drove on, praying that he would be safe.

The Russians, perhaps in fury because two of their men had been found dead, might do everything they could think of to destroy him before they would be obliged to leave Samosia because it was under British protection for ever.

'I love him! *I love him*!' she kept saying to herself in her mind.

The wheels of the carriage when they touched the hard roads of the City seemed to repeat the words over and over again.

In the short time she had given them to prepare for the marriage they had, to her delight, found a number of Union Jacks which were now flying from the windows of the houses they were passing.

To her surprise there was also a large brass band playing *God Save the Queen* in the Square outside the Cathedral.

It was exactly one minute to four o'clock when the carriage drew up outside the steps that led up to the West door of the large and ancient Cathedral of Samosia.

It had stood proudly there for many centuries and was revered by endless pilgrims from all over the Balkans, who would come to pray and present their offerings to the Patron Saint of Samosia, St. Demetrius.

The soldiers who had escorted them were joined by those waiting for Linetta's arrival at the Cathedral.

On what had obviously been their orders they stood in line and made a passage for her from her carriage to the West door.

The soldiers' bayonets were raised over her head so that it would be impossible for her to be fired at by an enemy.

As Linetta reached the West door with her mother and father behind her, the organ inside the Cathedral began to play a rousing march.

The ten bridesmaids were waiting for her looking like a bunch of roses themselves.

The two girls who were the daughters of the Count rushed up to her and she kissed them both.

She told them all how beautiful they were and how grateful she was.

"It is marvellous, absolutely marvellous," they kept saying over and over again.

As she moved up the aisle, the eldest girl put the bridesmaids into order and they followed Linetta as if they were part of her wedding gown.

A Verger walked slowly ahead of her and her father carrying a golden cross.

When they reached the choir, Linetta was at once aware that the Prince was waiting for her standing on the Chancel steps.

She had thrown back her veil before she left the carriage, so that all of the packed congregation could see her face.

She was wondering, as she moved forward on her father's arm, what the Prince was feeling.

She then looked down as if afraid to face him.

Only when she arrived at the altar and the Prince had come to her side did she raise her head.

It was then, just as she had been hoping, that she saw an incredulous and amazed expression in his eyes.

It was as if he could hardly believe that he was not dreaming.

He looked radiant in his ceremonial Army uniform in the light coming from the candles on the altar. There was a blue sash across his chest and his medals gleamed brightly.

He looked every inch a King.

Then he reached out his hand.

Although it was incorrect, Linetta slipped hers into his.

Almost as if she had known that this would happen, she had not only thrown back her veil before she entered the Cathedral but taken the gloves from her hands.

When he clasped her fingers so tightly that it was almost painful, she knew that he was just as thrilled and delighted as she wanted him to be because she was about to become his wife.

The Wedding Service was extremely moving and was beautifully conducted by the Archbishop of Samosia.

The prayers had a sincerity about them that made her feel as if they were carried from the Cathedral up into the clouds and into Heaven itself.

After the Prince had put the wedding ring on her finger and they knelt for the final blessing, the Archbishop and the five Priests with him solemnly began the prayers of the Coronation Service.

It was just a short Service, but one that astonished everyone in the Cathedral.

They could hardly believe what they were hearing.

As Linetta and the Prince moved down the aisle as man and wife and King and Queen, the choir burst into the Samosian National Anthem.

The strength and beauty of the notes continued until they had reached the West door.

It was then, because they had been told what was happening inside the Cathedral, that the vast crowd outside went mad with delight.

They cheered and cheered as they covered the bride and bridegroom with rose petals.

They were throwing every flower they could find in the square at their feet.

When they came to the last step down to the open carriage, which was waiting for them, the Prince raised his hand and there was complete silence from the hundreds of people gathered there.

He thanked them for coming to what he was sure would be a day they would always remember, which would go down in the history books.

"I am the luckiest and most blessed man in the world by marrying such a beautiful and intelligent English bride," he told the crowd. "She has not only saved this country from its enemies but has brought a new era to it in that it is now Royal."

He paused to look round at all the people listening to him before he went on,

"As King and Queen we will help to save not only ourselves but the whole of the Balkans from those who are trying so wickedly to destroy our independence and turn us into slaves."

There were huge cheers.

Then the Prince proclaimed,

"As King and Queen, we dedicate ourselves to you all. We pray that through our endeavours your children and, I hope, ours will find this a very much better world than it has ever been before."

Now the men in the crowd were waving their hats and the women their handkerchiefs, as they cheered until they were hoarse.

"Together," the Prince continued, "we now intend to make Samosia great. Not only here at home but to help all those who are persecuted and threatened."

He turned and smiled at Linetta.

"I believe in peace," he said, "and, when I achieve it, I will fight with my heart and soul to rid ourselves of the evil of those who through greed want to take away from us that which is ours, that which we were given by God when we were born."

Again he paused before he finished emphatically,

"What is ours is ours and will remain so if you will fight for your children as my wife and I will, so that they will all grow up in peace and, if we really use our brains, prosperity."

There were wild cheers as the Prince's speech came to an end.

As Linetta and he stepped into an open carriage, the horses moved slowly away from the square followed by the crowds of those accompanying them.

They were once again proudly singing the National Anthem of Samosia and then to Linetta's and the Prince's delight, they broke into a rousing *God Save the Queen.*

The noise of the people's cheers and singing made it quite impossible for the Prince and Linetta to speak.

They merely held hands and raised the other hand in answer to the cheers and excitement of the crowd.

When they eventually reached The Palace and the carriage stopped, the Prince jumped out and helped Linetta down the steps.

Then he turned to her and said very softly so that only she could hear,

"I am now completely sure that I must be dreaming, my darling."

"If you are dreaming, then I am certainly dreaming too," Linetta whispered.

She looked up into his eyes as she spoke.

For a moment neither of them could move.

As they went into The Palace to be joined a few moments later by Linetta's parents and a large number of dignitaries, there was no further chance of them talking to each other.

There was an endless supply of champagne to drink their health with and it was poured out liberally by a small army of attendants.

Also there was an enormous wedding cake that had been made by the chefs at The Palace as soon as they learnt that there was to be a Royal Wedding.

*

It was late before anyone made a move to leave The Palace and all the festivities.

When they did, the Prince said,

"My wife and I are exceedingly grateful for your congratulations and good wishes and that you came to our Wedding."

There was a respectful silence before he smiled and went on,

"But, as we have both had a very long and arduous day, I now insist on my wife retiring and I know you will understand if we now bid you goodnight and go to our own Private Apartments."

There was clapping and cheering after he had said this.

Then, when they were just on the point of moving away, there were cries of,

"God bless the bride and God bless you both now and for ever."

Linetta put her arm through the Prince's.

As they walked up the stairs together, he said,

"I still think I am dreaming. How could you have deceived me so cleverly, my darling."

"I had to decide whether or not I would marry you," Linetta replied. "I could not contemplate marrying a man I had never seen."

"You played your role as Governess to the Count's children so very cleverly, *Miss Lane*, and you completely deceived me and even so I fell madly in love with you," the Prince answered, "but we will talk about it later."

They had reached her bedroom by this time and he added,

"We have now been crowned the King and Queen of Samosia thanks to you, my darling, but I feel more that we have been crowned by music, your wonderful music that is not of this world."

She saw that there were two maids waiting inside the help her out of her wedding dress.

The Prince went to his own room which was next door.

Because they realised that she wanted to be quiet, the maids undressed her quickly and then helped Linetta into one of the beautiful nightgowns that her mother had bought for her in France.

The maids left her after murmuring,

"Goodnight and God bless Your Majesty."

Linetta walked to the window.

As she expected, the moon was turning the garden to silver.

The many fountains were still throwing their water up into the sky.

There was a full moon and the stars were coming out.

It was so beautiful that she felt almost as if it really was just a dream and so could not be happening to her.

Then suddenly, as she had not heard him entering the room, the Prince was at her side.

For a moment they looked into each other's eyes and did not speak.

Then he said in a voice that seemed strange even to Linetta,

"You are so lovely, so perfect and so exactly what I asked the wishing well to give me, but I still don't believe you are true."

He put his hand over hers as he went on,

"I feel you may fly away into the sky and become one of the angels and I will never find you again."

"I am yours," Linetta sighed gently. "I promise I will never leave you."

"That is all I want to hear," her husband answered. "Oh, my darling, how could you have been so clever and so brave not only to save my life but to leave me without the slightest idea that you were the marvellous bride who was to save my country and me from destruction?"

"I had to see you first even though I knew that it was my duty to save Samosia," Linetta said in a low voice.

She smiled as she went on,

"But when I saw you for the first time I knew that you meant something more to me than any man could."

Her voice dropped to little more than a whisper as she said,

"When you kissed me, I knew that I had found the love I had always prayed for which I thought I would never have."

"I felt exactly the same," the Prince replied. "I was marrying for my country and from the first moment I saw you I knew that you meant something very special to me that no woman has ever done."

He drew in a deep breath before he went on,

"But when I kissed you I knew you were everything I had ever dreamt of, believed in or prayed for. Oh, my precious, my darling one, how could we have ever been so lucky? How could we have been able to find each other when under the circumstances it seemed so impossible that we should?"

He pulled Linetta to him as he spoke.

Then his lips were on hers.

He was kissing her wildly and passionately.

At the same time he felt that he had found the Holy Grail and it was his for ever.

*

A long time later they moved into the huge bed that was ornamented with golden cupids, birds and butterflies.

As the Prince carried Linetta from the window, he set her down very gently against the pillows.

Then, blowing out all the candles round the bed, he joined her.

He did, however, leave the curtain open.

The magical moonlight came streaming in through the window making the room, the Prince thought, feel as it had when Linetta had played the piano to him.

To Linetta it was as if the angels themselves had come down to encircle them both with the real love that only comes from God.

Then, as the Prince drew her even closer to him and his kisses grew more demanding, the touch of his hands made Linetta feel as if he drew her heart from her body and made it his.

"I love you! I adore you, Ivor," she whispered not once but time after time.

Then he said in a voice which hardly sounded like his,

"You are mine, now and for ever. Oh, my darling Linetta, how could God have been so kind to us both?"

As he kissed her wildly, then very gently, so as not to frighten her, he made her his.

It was then at that moment of sublime rapture that Linetta knew they had reached Heaven, the Heaven that so graciously had brought them together.

It had given them the Love that came from God, was part of God and was theirs for Eternity and beyond.